"LOOK OUT!"

The warning came just in time. The Cheyenne on the army horse pounded through the camp, scattering men and horses, his eyes fixed on Rafferty.

Mountain Star threw himself from his horse and slammed into Rafferty's back. Both men hit the ground, and Mountain Star was the first to his feet. He produced a long-bladed knife and dove at Rafferty, who sat dazed on the ground.

Mountain Star never saw the pistol in Malone's hand. Malone cracked down hard, catching the Cheyenne flush on the skull and the warrior fell like a sandbag, lying motionless against the earth...

EASY COMPANY

EASY COMPANY

AND THE LONG MARCHERS

COMPANY

JOHN WESLEY HOWARD

A JOVE BOOK

EASY COMPANY AND THE LONG MARCHERS

A Jove book / published by arrangement with
the author

PRINTING HISTORY
Jove edition / May 1982

ISBN:0-515-06033-X

Jove books are published by Jove Publications, Inc.,
200 Madison Avenue, New York, N. Y. 10016.
The words "A JOVE BOOK" and the 𝕁 with sunburst
are trademarks belonging to Jove Publications, Inc.

PRINTED IN THE UNITED STATES OF AMERICA

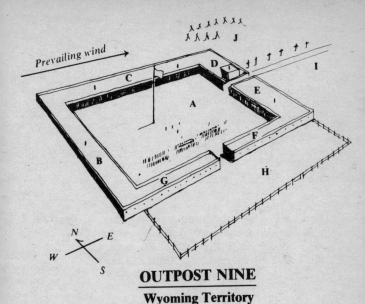

Prevailing wind →

N E W S (compass)

OUTPOST NINE

Wyoming Territory

KEY

A. Parade and flagstaff

B. Officers' quarters ("officers' country")

C. Enlisted men's quarters: barracks, day room, and mess

D. Kitchen, quartermaster supplies, ordnance shop, guardhouse

E. Suttler's store and other shops, tack room, and smithy

F. Stables

G. Quarters for dependents and guests; communal kitchen

H. Paddock

I. Road and telegraph line to regimental headquarters

J. Indian camp occupied by transient "friendlies"

INTERIOR   OUTSIDE

OUTPOST NUMBER NINE
(DETAIL)

Outpost Number Nine is a typical High Plains military outpost of the days following the Battle of the Little Big Horn, and is the home of Easy Company. It is not a "fort"; an official fort is the headquarters of a regiment. However, it resembles a fort in its construction.

The birdseye view shows the general layout and orientation of Outpost Number Nine; features are explained in the Key.

The detail shows a cross-section through the outpost's double walls, which ingeniously combine the functions of fortification and shelter.

The walls are constructed of sod, dug from the prairie on which Outpost Number Nine stands, and are sturdy enough to withstand an assault by anything less than artillery. The roof is of log beams covered by planking, tarpaper, and a top layer of sod. It also provides a parapet from which the outpost's defenders can fire down on an attacking force.

one ————————————

Smoke rose in a wind-buffeted column from the dry plains. The weary bay horse beneath Lieutenant Matt Kincaid shifted its feet impatiently and blew. Kincaid held up a hand and the patrol behind him eased toward the rim of the low knoll.

Windy Mandalian, the civilian scout, lowered the brass-bound telescope from his eye and, without speaking, handed it to Kincaid, who adjusted the eyepiece, bringing the source of the smoke into sharp focus.

Six immigrant wagons lined the road below the army patrol. To one side, the owners of the wagons were herded into a tight knot, their women and children among them. Raiders were going through the wagons, throwing out booty to be searched by others standing on the ground.

Two mounted men sat at the perimeter of the action, eyes scanning the long plains. The smoke, which had been billowing up from an overturned prairie schooner, was now diminishing and, drifted by the wind, it screened the scene intermittently from Kincaid's scrutiny. He handed the telescope back to Windy.

"Blodgett?" Sergeant Olsen asked.

"It is. And the bastard's gotten too confident this time. Take six men down the wash, Gus," he told the sergeant. "When we hit them, they'll likely try for the coulees. See that they don't make it."

1

"They won't," Gus Olsen promised. It was a grim vow; Olsen had seen too much of Hal Blodgett's work—butchery and rapaciousness that could match the worst Cheyenne attacks. He preyed on the unsuspecting bands of immigrant families drifting into Wyoming.

Blodgett's usual method was simply to drift up and offer his services as a scout. The immigrants, unfamiliar with the territory, gratefully accepted. Then this would happen.

Gus glanced toward the wagon train once more, lifted his hand, and silently led his six men down into the concealing dry wash.

The willows were gray with weather, thick and dry. Insects hummed among the swamp brush along the cut. The horses beneath them made only a faint, whispery sound as Olsen's party moved southward, invisible from the flats above.

Private Malone shifted in his saddle, wiping his throat with a spare handkerchief. Sweat trickled down his chest. His shirt clung to his heated body. He carried his Springfield across his saddlebows.

"Look at him," McBride said to Malone. "Damned if I know what he's doing here."

Malone squinted into the sun and studied the new man, Herman Javitts by name. He had the thin face of a ferret, and utterly pale skin that seemed to be drawn back from his eternally surprised eyes.

"That's a soldier?" McBride asked.

Gus Olsen looked back sharply. It was no time for conversation, and Reb McBride fell silent. Javitts blinked at the two men who had momentarily studied him, then turned his head away.

It was damnably hot in the coulee, where no trace of breeze reached the patrol. He was perspiring copiously. His hands were damp, and he had to wipe them continually on his pants.

The horse misstepped beneath him, crossing a field of stones, and Javitts's head snapped back. Regaining

2

his balance, he glanced around to see if anyone had noticed, but he could not read their dark, tanned faces.

They were intent now on the battle to come. Javitts took a deep breath. The close air in the coulee seemed devoid of oxygen. He realized suddenly that his arms and legs were trembling.

His stomach knotted and rolled over slowly. *I'm scared sick,* he told himself. But there was nothing to be done about it. He gripped the reins still tighter and rode on as if through a nightmare, the sun glaring down, his body shaking itself to pieces, his mouth dry.

Gus Olsen dismounted and clambered up the hot, sandy bank of the coulee. Removing his hat, he peered up through the screen of twisted brush. Satisfied, he slid back down in a cloud of dust.

"Spread it out. Three north, three south. Keep fifty yards between you." Olsen had gathered up the reins to his stocky bay horse before he added, "Don't give these cutthroats any breaks, men. They've done worse than you or I could imagine. If there's any doubt, kill 'em."

Gus watched as his men silently filtered through the brush. Then he ground-tethered his horse and crawled back up to the rim of the wash, his Springfield rifle warm in his hands.

He could see the wagon train, two hundred yards away, quite clearly. His line of sight toward Lieutenant Kincaid was cut off, but he didn't need to see Kincaid. By watching Blodgett, he'd damn sure know when the lieutenant had begun his charge.

A red ant crawled across Gus's hand, and he blew it away. The cicadas in the wash below kept up a constant, shrill singing. The sand beneath him was hot; the day was breathless.

As he watched, a man, possibly protesting the mistreatment of a woman, was hammered to the ground by two of Blodgett's men. A harsh laugh carried across the distance between the wagon looters and Olsen.

Then it happened. A big man with a massive black

3

beard lifted a hand toward the north, and the looters dropped their booty and raced toward the horses.

"This way now," Olsen breathed. "Make your run this way, Blodgett."

To the south and east lay only open prairie. It made sense for Blodgett and his cutthroats to make for the network of coulees to the west, but Olsen held his breath until the first horse was turned in his direction and a shouted command brought all eight of the looters around.

Gus snuggled down, drawing back the hammer of his Springfield. His unholstered Schofield Smith & Wesson revolver lay at hand. Again, Olsen silently cursed the bumbling bureaucrats in Washington who issued these single-shot Springfields to the army while the Indians at the agencies were armed with repeaters.

A shot cracked across the plains, and another, and Olsen saw a looter stand straight up in his stirrups, slap at his throat, and topple over, to be dragged a hundred yards by his panicked horse before his boot slipped free of the stirrup.

Now he could see Kincaid's force, hear the crackling of their rifle fire, and another looter went down, his roan cartwheeling, throwing him free. That left six, and they charged toward the coulees, their horses throwing up plumes of dust.

They turned in their saddles, fired, and dug their spurs into their horses. The earth rumbled beneath Olsen now, and he settled in, sighting in on the chest of the man nearest him. He was a hundred yards away and closing fast. He wore a black coat and a faded red shirt with silver buttons. Gus sighted in on the second button below his throat, took a breath, released it halfway, and triggered off.

The Springfield slapped smartly against his shoulder, and a cloud of black-powder smoke blossomed forth and drifted away. When it cleared, there was no sign of the man in the red shirt. His roan horse, frothing at the mouth, eyes wide, pounded forward in a blind, panicked run.

Gus switched his sights, heard a shot from up the coulee, saw his target go down, and selected another. The remaining looters fanned out, riding low across the withers.

Their situation was desperate, and they knew it. The patrol behind them was closing the gap, and now, in sight of the coulees, they found themselves caught in a crossfire.

Gus saw a looter try to turn his horse, to wheel and run south, but he was too late. A heavy Springfield .45-70 slug had taken his horse in the shoulder, and as he tried to leap free, the horse rolled and crushed him. His bellow of pain hung in the air, but Olsen felt no sympathy for the man who had broken others, heard others cry out, pleading for mercy.

He was there suddenly. Blodgett himself, riding low on the side of his horse, Indian-fashion. Gus hadn't responded quickly enough. His eyes had been on the falling rider, and he had just seen Blodgett's big gray gelding out of the corner of his eye. It had been easy to mistake the horse for a riderless one, and Olsen cursed himself for the mistake.

He leaped to his feet, raising his Scoff. He followed Blodgett's horse with the front bead and fired twice. The gray never even broke stride, and as Gus scrambled up out of the coulee, Blodgett rode the gray up and into a tangle of willow brush.

Malone was the nearest man, and Olsen called out above the battle sounds.

"Malone! It's Blodgett, coming to you!"

Gus ran toward his horse, half running, half falling down the bank of the coulee. He mounted the bay at a dead run, heeling the horse hard.

He charged into the head-high willow brush and then slowed his horse. He stopped, listening, realizing that he had put himself in a bad situation. He was grateful that he had experienced men with him, men who wouldn't turn and fire at any unexpected sound.

The gunfire had faded away and now the day fell

5

silent. No wind stirred in the tall brush. The sweat ran from Gus's forehead into his eyes. Still he did not move. He sat listening, his eyes combing the brush below him.

And then he saw a flash of dappled gray, briefly through a gap in the brush. He raised his pistol, but the horse was gone again, swallowed up by the silver-gray willows.

Gus eased his horse downslope, fighting through a tangle of blackthorn and nopal cactus. Reaching the coulee bottom, he found it empty. Casting about from side to side, he found a single indistinct hoofprint in the loose sand. He couldn't even be certain that it had been made recently, and there were no others. The sand lost the impressions almost as soon as they were made.

Slowly he walked his bay southward, hearing another horse, far to the north, whinny. Gus placed his hand over his own horse's nose, preventing it from responding to the reflex to answer.

It was dry, hot. The sun seemed to scrape at the back of his neck. He wiped the perspiration from his eyes and rode on, his eyes searching the rising bluffs on either side.

"I've lost the son of a bitch," he muttered.

No one in the world could blame Gus Olsen for not taking Hal Blodgett, but he blamed himself. The man was an animal, not fit to live, and they had had him in their hands only to see him slip away. Of course, he still might be there, hidden in the coulee, but Olsen knew that the longer he was missing, the greater was the chance that he had made his escape.

He rounded a turn in the coulee and stopped abruptly.

Malone was crouched above him on a sandy ledge, his pistol in his hand, a finger to his lips, and Olsen nodded, his eyes straining to see whatever it was Malone saw.

And Malone damn sure saw something. He crept forward now as Olsen watched him, hatless, moving in a crouch, his cocked pistol uplifted.

6

Malone's feet were soundless against the sand. He moved nearer to the edge of the sandy bench, careful not to go too near. The slightest sound, the whisper of sand trickling over the lip, might alert the man below him.

And that man was Hal Blodgett. Malone had seen him moving as silently as a ghost through the towering willows. Slipping from his post, Malone had followed him the quarter of a mile down the coulee to where the wash dead-ended.

Blodgett was still mounted, but he was sagging badly in the saddle, gripping his arm as he leaned forward. He'd been hit, but Blodgett was still a dangerous man. He held a Colt revolver in his injured hand, the hammer drawn back. His black eyes flickered toward the brush from time to time, a virulent savagery in them.

Malone glanced behind him and saw that Gus had slipped from the saddle, but was holding his position. That blocked any escape that way. There was a way through the brush, leading toward the eastern rim, but Malone doubted that Blodgett could even see it from where he sat.

Malone took another step and then froze, a curse curling his lips. Javitts was there suddenly, standing before Hal Blodgett. Where in hell had Herman come from!

The little man was trembling as he stood holding his gun on the looter chief. His face was washed out, his eyes wide and uncertain.

"Drop the gun, Blodgett," Private Javitts said, his voice squeaking uncontrollably. "Drop it and let's go in quietly."

"Sure," Malone heard Blodgett say, but there was a cold, warning edge to his tone and Malone tensed, ready to leap.

It was already too late. As Malone watched, Herman Javitts flinched and the big, bearded man touched off his Colt nearly in the soldier's face. Roweling his big gray ferociously, Blodgett drove the shoulder of his horse into Javitts, and the little man, stunned by the near miss of

Blodgett's Colt, went down in a heap, the gray trampling over him, bucking into the heavy brush as Malone, firing as he slid from the bluff, winged four shots after him. All misses.

Malone hit the flat running, but already Blodgett was gone. He heard Olsen's horse racing toward them, but Malone knew Blodgett would not be caught again, not this day.

Angrily, Malone shoved his pistol into his holster and walked to where Herman Javitts lay sprawled on the sand.

Malone hooked Javitts under the arm and pulled him roughly to his knees. Javitts groaned and looked up pitiably. "God, Malone. I'm hurt."

"You ought to be dead!" Malone said bluntly.

"I think my arm's broke."

Malone tore open Javitts's shirt and looked at the arm. Testing it more roughly than he had to, he decided that it wasn't broken, but only badly bruised where Blodgett's horse had run into him.

Javitts's face was a mess. Burned red and black by the muzzle flash and gunpowder grains, it was puffed badly around the left eye from his fall.

"I thought I was a dead man," Javitts groaned. "When he fired into my face . . ." He shuddered.

Malone only scowled. At the sound of the approaching horse, he turned and saw Olsen rounding the bend at a hard gallop.

Malone waved his arms in signal and shouted, "That way, Gus!" although he knew the looter had enough of a lead that they would never catch him now.

Turning back, he once again studied Herman Javitts. The little man was miserable—shaken, hurt, and numbed. Malone squinted his eyes tightly and shook his head, then said to Javitts, "Come on. I'll walk you back to your horse. We'll wash your face and see how bad it really is."

Meekly, Javitts accepted Malone's help. Malone slipped an arm around his waist and guided the unsteady soldier back through the brush toward his horse. Now Malone could see Kincaid along the rim; he could see the soldiers beating the brush, searching with fading expectations for Hal Blodgett.

Malone, panting badly, climbed the hill again and found Javitts's horse. Letting the little man slide to a sitting position, he retrieved his canteen from his saddle. Taking a deep drink himself, Malone turned to Javitts.

"Give me your scarf," Malone said sourly. Javitts untied it slowly, his hands trembling, and handed it to the veteran soldier.

"You're mad?" Javitts asked in a way that was more statement than question.

"Goddamn right," Malone grumbled. He poured water onto the scarf and began mopping Javitts's burned face. "I had the son of a bitch in my sights and he got away. Thanks to you."

"I didn't know you were up there," Javitts protested. Malone rubbed a bit too hard, and he winced. "I was trying to do my job, trying to capture him."

"You damn near got your head blown off, Javitts!"

"What was I supposed to do?" Javitts was nearly crying with frustration.

"Shoot the bastard cold, that's what I was going to do," Malone answered. He sat back on his heels, putting the canteen aside. "You look like hell."

"Shoot him! Murder him!"

"That's it."

"In cold blood?"

"You're goddamn right," Malone said viciously. He stood and hooked the canteen back on the bay's saddle. Malone had to look away briefly; his anger was flaring up again. He saw Gus returning on a lathered horse, saw Reb McBride leading his own horse and Malone's toward them. Kincaid was scanning the horizon with Windy Mandalian's telescope.

"I couldn't do that," Javitts said softly. "Just kill him, like a rabid dog."

"That's what he is. Only worse. A rabid dog's sick.

Hal Blodgett is just rotten. He kills for the fun of it. Women, kids . . . and now there'll be more dead because we let him get through us."

"He hasn't got a gang left." Herman said, rising slowly. He made an odd, childish shrug with his hands.

"There's always more recruits," Malone told him coldly. "It was Blodgett we had to get. And we didn't."

Reb McBride had arrived with the horses, and he looked to be in no better spirits than Malone was. He looked from Malone to Javitts and back, and asked in a drawl, "You two havin' fun?"

"Lot of fun, Corp," Malone said, and the bugler nodded his head. When Malone called him 'corporal,' it was a bad sign.

"He all right?" Reb asked, nodding at the burned, battered man beside Malone.

"I don't know." Malone swung heavily into the saddle, tugging his hat low against the dying sun. "I don't know if the man is all right or not, Reb. I truly don't."

Reb frowned, glanced once again at Javitts, and then swung his own horse, following Malone up the sandy bluff to form up on Gus Olsen, who was just finishing his report to Lieutenant Kincaid.

"Well, he's wounded," Kincaid was saying. "There's still a chance we can kick him out of that brush."

Windy looked unconvinced. He leaned his head away and spat a stream of tobacco juice. Then he straightened and, with a slight shake of his head, once again studied the maze of coulees, the wide plains beyond. If they had a hundred men, they couldn't search all that land and hope to find him.

"Mebbe he's hit hard enough to bleed to death for us," Windy cracked.

"No such luck," Malone said.

Kincaid's head swiveled toward the private. "Did you see him, Malone?"

"Right up close, sir." Briefly he explained what had happened in the coulee. Matt Kincaid took it all in with-

10

out changing expression. Herman Javitts was just now beginning to climb out of the wash; he looked as if he had been set on fire and beaten out with shovels.

Kincaid could attach no blame to the man. He hadn't acted cowardly. No, Javitts couldn't be faulted for anything except not being brutal enough, and you don't discipline a man for that.

"Too bad he doesn't know Blodgett as we do," Kincaid said to no one in particular.

Kincaid himself had seen the bandit's work, close up. You don't forget a woman who has been raped, brutalized, and murdered in front of her baby, sitting in the dirt nearby, screaming. Kincaid thought of himself as a compassionate man, one who deplored unnecessary violence. But killing a dog like Hal Blodgett was not unnecessary violence.

Aloud he said, "Spread them out, Gus. Let's sweep through the coulees by sections. Send out four flankers to watch the plains in case he breaks out. Windy, find a perch and put that glass to work. You can't track him out of that, can you?"

"Don't believe I could track a herd of buffalo across that sand, Matt. I'll find me a spot."

Windy took his telescope back, wheeled his fine big Appaloosa, and rode southward, the wind riffling the fringes of his buckskin jacket.

Matt Kincaid turned his horse and rode at a soft canter back toward the immigrant train. Goods were being reloaded onto the wagons by grim-faced men. A woman stood disgustedly over a smashed trunk. Dresses and household goods lay scattered across the plains, dropped by the bandits in their haste.

A baldheaded man with a foot-long white beard was perched on an upturned bucket, having the gash on his head tended by a woman in gingham.

"Get 'em?" the man asked as Kincaid walked his horse toward the wagon.

"All but one." Matt swung down, dusting his uniform.

"I just wanted to see if anyone needed medical help. We haven't got a surgeon at Outpost Nine, but—"

"We'll make it."

Matt turned toward the sharp voice. She stood there long and spicy, eyes sparking, a spanking new Winchester in her hands, eyeing him with sharp displeasure.

"Ma'am." Matt touched his hatbrim, smiling faintly.

Who did this firebrand belong to? She was a beautiful woman, no two ways about it, with long dark hair, half pinned up now; she had flaring, compelling hips and a full, tempting mouth, but there was evil temper in her eyes.

"Katie—" the baldheaded man began, but she interrupted him.

"We don't need your help, Lieutenant—is that what you are?—not from the army."

"Is something wrong?" Matt asked dryly. The bald man smiled faintly at that.

"You're damned right there is," the girl snapped.

"No need to talk like that," the older woman commented. She had finished bandaging her husband's head, and now she bent to kiss his cheek lightly.

"Now, Katie," the man began again. "The gentleman is only trying to help us."

"Like they helped us before!"

Kincaid was puzzled. "I don't understand—"

"You were watching. You knew they were here. Yet you waited up on that hill until my uncle had been beaten, and Mr. Jessop—quite badly, I might add—and then you came down. Don't deny it, I saw you."

"There were reasons," Matt said, suddenly irritated. He was damned if he'd explain his reasons to this hellion.

"You just *used* us. As bait for your trap."

Matt said nothing. His jaw muscle twitched with annoyance. The old man moved toward the girl, trying to soothe her. He whispered something into her pretty pink ear and turned her away, but not before she had time to add, "I think the whole army . . . stinks!"

Matt had to grin despite himself and the girl, and seeing the grin turned the girl's face crimson with anger. She stalked away, back rigid, still gripping that rifle with both hands.

"She's probably right," Matt said, shaking his head. "It does give off an unhealthy odor at times." He turned to the man with the bandaged head, "But as for us using you as bait—"

"No need to explain, sir," the man replied. "Hell, she's just good and mad, good and scared. We come close to being hit real hard. Wasn't for you, we would have been. You see, she lost her ma and pa to some white wagon train bandits not a year back. Katie, she hasn't got over it yet."

"I understand," Matt said. He glanced toward the wagon where the girl had disappeared. When he looked back, her uncle was smiling.

"She's a good-looking thing, ain't she?"

"Norm!" his wife exclaimed.

"Well, she is. But she don't take to blue uniforms, Lieutenant . . ."

"Kincaid," Matt supplied. They shook hands.

"Norm Braun. Hell of it is, she'll be seeing nothing but blue uniforms where we're going."

"Oh?"

Braun nodded, refastening the harness on his team. "I'm headin' up to Fort Robinson, I'm the new sutler there. My other brother, Abraham, he's cashing it in. Tired of the plains, the Oglala, and the army life, I suppose. Thought I'd give it a try."

"Good luck to you," Matt said. "You'll be all right?"

"Yes, sir. Thank you—I appreciate what you've done, even if certain other members of this train don't." He glanced toward his wagon, the corner of his mouth lifting in a smile.

They shook hands again, and Matt swung into the saddle. The day was already late, the shadows growing long. He could see Gus Olsen far to the south, breaking

13

up out of the coulee, and from Gus's movements—quick, irritable—Matt could tell there had been no luck.

Mandalian confirmed it. "Nothin'. The son of a bitch is slippery."

Matt glanced toward the skies, which were already darkening as the sun wheeled toward the mountains far to the west. "We'll keep at it until dark, Windy. After that, there's not much point to it, is there?"

"Not a hell of a lot," Windy had to agree.

The wagon train was rolling on now, and both men watched as the laboring oxen ambled northward, drawing the prairie schooners behind them. The figures became smaller and more indistinct as distance and shadow swallowed them up.

"Thought mebbe they'd offer to cook supper for us," Windy groused. Matt smiled faintly. They hadn't been quite *that* grateful.

Together the two men rode southward along the rim of the deeply shadowed coulee. Dove winged homeward across the leaden skies. The soldiers working the heavy brush below were lost in shadow. Only the creaking of their saddles and an occasional smothered curse could be heard.

Gus Olsen rode up to meet them. He saluted Matt stiffly, then wiped his sweatband with his scarf, mopped his brush-scratched face, and shook his head.

"Not a sign of the bastard, sir."

Matt had been turned away, still watching the distant wagon train. Windy was studying him with faint puzzlement. Matt nodded abruptly.

"Call 'em in, Gus," he said heavily. "We lost him in full daylight, so we'll never find Hal Blodgett in the dark."

Malone staggered into camp, carrying his saddle. McBride was sitting near the wind-drifted fire on his McClellan, cupping his tin coffee cup in both hands. He looked drawn, exhausted. Working through that brush was an ordeal. Stretch Dobbs had been poked in the eye by a twig, and was having it looked at by Windy. Trueblood was already asleep, flat on his back with no blanket.

"Never mind a cup, just hand me the pot," Malone said as he sat to the fire. McBride hardly smiled. Malone poured himself a cup of bitter, black coffee, sipped it, and frowned in disgust. He had really wanted that coffee, but it was bad, alkali-tasting.

"Y'ever think of raising sheep?" McBride asked.

Malone placed his hat aside and yawned, answering, "Anything but this. What do you think we got in our skulls, Reb? Can't be brains."

"Can't be," Reb agreed. He threw the dregs of his coffee into the fire, producing a steaming hiss. Then he settled back, using his saddle as a pillow.

Malone took another sip of his coffee, made a wry face, and considered throwing it out. A shadow fell across the earth at his feet; glancing up, he saw the discolored face of Herman Javitts. Nervously the little man poured himself a cup of coffee. Then he sat cross-legged on the ground, watching Trueblood, who snorted and rolled over in his sleep, his hand clenching and unclenching.

Finally he spoke, "I'm sorry, Malone."

"'S all right," Malone grumbled.

"It's just that I've never killed a man."

"No?" Malone's eyebrows arched in mild surprise.

"Oh, I know I'll have to. We'll get into an Indian skirmish and I'll have no choice."

"Think you can do it?" Malone wanted to know. Javitts didn't answer; he looked away toward the fire, and Malone went on, "If you can't, you'd best find a way to get out of Wyoming, out of the army."

"If I had to..." Javitts nervously pulled at his nose. "It's just that I was standing there, looking into Blodgett's eyes. A man's eyes. A life is sacred to me, Malone. My father was a preacher, you know, and I learned that— a man's life is sacred!"

"Should be," Malone agreed harshly. "But there's nothing sacred about a butcher like Blodgett. You should have killed him, Herman. Damned if you shouldn't have."

Malone poured his coffee out onto the ground, snatched up his blanket, and walked into the darkness, away from the halo of campfire light.

Javitts sat there silently, watching the flames long after the others were asleep. A coyote howled far in the distance, and Javitts buried his face in his trembling hands. Damn them all! He'd not become a killer. He'd do his duty, fight if he had to, but he'd not kill unnecessarily. There was always another way, always. Even out here. The fire burned low, flickered, and went out, and still Herman Javitts sat there, watching the golden glow of the embers far into the cold and empty night.

two ═══════════════════

The sun was already high in the sky when the patrol trailed into Outpost Number Nine. Odd, Matt Kincaid thought, how this godforsaken pile of timbers and sod, so wretched and dismal, could look inviting, warm, and comfortable on the way home. *Home,* he laughed inwardly. Yet that was the association, ludicrous as it was. Outpost Number Nine, with its squat sod walls, dusty and hot in summer, damp and cold in winter, was home.

The gates swung wide and they streamed through, weary, hungry, and dirty.

Matt Kincaid swung down in front of headquarters, handed the reins of his horse to Gus Olsen, and stepped up onto the plankwalk. He tried to dust his uniform off and crease his hat a little, then he stepped into the orderly room.

"Welcome back, sir," Sergeant Ben Cohen said warmly. He saluted and then offered his thick hand to Kincaid, who shook it.

"No casualties," Kincaid said immediately, knowing that was the question uppermost in all their minds. You just didn't get used to seeing your friends and comrades-in-arms come back draped over their saddles, and "no casualties" was enough to produce a smile of relief every time.

"Coffee, sir?" Cohen asked, but Kincaid declined.

Later, maybe. Coffee, a bath, and some of Dutch Rothausen's buffalo stew—he had smelled it a quarter of a mile out. Then sleep. Hours of blessed sleep. But right now it was time for business.

"He's in there," Cohen said, nodding toward Captain Conway's office.

Kincaid removed his hat and stepped to the door. Rapping, he was summoned, and he stepped into Conway's office.

"Any luck?" Conway asked without preliminaries.

"Some," Kincaid answered.

"Sit down and tell me about it, Matt. Have a drink?"

"No, thank you, sir. I'd fall asleep before I finished my report."

Conway nodded. Kincaid was exhausted, his eyes redrimmed, his face taut. He'd have about six hours to get over that, Conway thought with regret. He poured himself a glass of whiskey from the bottle in his desk drawer, leaned back comfortably, and listened as Kincaid reported.

"Damned shame he got away. Think he was bleeding badly enough to kick off for us?"

"I only hope so, sir," Matt answered. There was something else on the captain's mind; Matt could see it. His eyes had been on Kincaid the whole time, but there was a certain look of half-attentiveness in them. "You want to tell me about it now?" he asked.

Conway grinned, "Am I that transparent?"

"We've been together a long while, sir."

"A long while." Conway smiled and was briefly silent. Then he rose and walked to stand before the wall map of the territory, as he frequently did when organizing his thoughts. "We're going to have to ride out this evening, Matt."

"Oh?" Kincaid frowned.

"And when I say 'we,' I mean damned near all of us."

"Trouble?" Kincaid was immediately intense.

"Not in the battle sense. I received a message from Regiment this morning. The Northern Cheyenne have surrendered. Two bands of them are to be escorted to Fort Robinson to be resettled. We're to relieve a detachment from Fort Keogh and watch them until we, in turn, are relieved by a force from Fort Laramie. *They* will turn them over to a detachment out of Fort Robinson."

"Fort Robinson." Matt nodded absently and Conway, perplexed, studied his lieutenant.

"Yes. As you know, they've got an Oglala agency there, and the Northern Cheyenne have close blood ties with the Oglala. They should be content there, relatively speaking. Not so much agency-jumping as they usually have with the newly resettled tribes. Matt, are you listening?"

"Yes, sir. Just a little more tired than I thought, I suspect." He had been listening, had heard every word the captain said, but somehow his attention had been less than perfect after Conway had mentioned Fort Robinson. He had experienced a vivid and unwarranted recollection of Katie Braun, tall, defiant, lovely. It was to Fort Robinson that she and her uncle were traveling. "We won't be going into Fort Robinson?" he asked casually.

Conway cocked his head curiously. Matt *was* tired; his eyes were distant, his mouth soft and slack. "No, Matt. I told you, we'll take over from the boys out of Keogh and escort them near the North Platte, to the troops from Laramie. We'll have them for a couple of hundred miles, that's all. I think," he said rising, "you had better eat and crawl into the sack. Fitzgerald should be in the BOQ—he just came off of OD. Will you send him over?"

"Yes, sir," Matt said, coming to his feet. He saluted smartly and turned on his heel, but Conway still had the feeling he had been speaking to a sleepwalker. He shook his head and returned to his desk, determined to try to push through still another request for replacement officers. The ones he had were working themselves into a stupor.

Kincaid had his shirt off before he reached his bunk. Second Lieutenant Fitzgerald was shaving when Matt stumbled in, and Fitz heard him mutter that the captain wanted to see him. Turning, his dark eyes sparkling, Fitzgerald watched as Matt tugged off his boots and flopped back on his bunk, eyes open, staring at the ceiling.

"What's up, Matt?" he asked, toweling off his face.

"We're going to escort some Cheyenne toward Fort Robinson."

"Oh?" Fitzgerald shrugged and found his cleanest tunic. Pulling it on, he studied Matt Kincaid more closely. There was a preoccupied man, Fitz thought, but he said nothing else to Matt after asking about casualties.

Fitzgerald picked up his hat, formed it, and planted it on his head. Then he went out, softly closing the door. Across the parade, Corporal Wojensky was just dismissing his firewood detail. Flora Conway was shaking a rug from the boardwalk in front of her quarters, and the captain's lady gave him a jaunty wave, adding a bright, friendly smile. Fitzgerald waved back and strode on.

The company clerk was alone in the outer office, and Fitzgerald smiled at the sight of Four Eyes Bradshaw, so engrossed in his paperwork that he hadn't even noticed the officer entering. Lieutenant Taylor liked to clear his throat or bang the door just to see Four Eyes leap to flustered attention, but Fitzgerald let the man work and walked on through to the captain's office, rapping on the doorframe.

Ben Cohen came to his feet briefly, and Conway nodded.

"Matt brief you, Fitz?"

"Sort of. The man was a bit vague, sir," Fitzgerald said with a grin.

20

"He was damned tired," Conway agreed.

"That too." Conway looked up, awaiting an explanation, and Fitzgerald went on with a grin, "He's showing the symptoms, sir. A married man might not notice it, but he's showing all the signs, plain enough to another lonely bachelor out on these damned plains—Lieutenant Kincaid has somewhere, some way, run across a woman."

"He didn't mention it."

"No, he wouldn't. But I'll weasel it out of him, sir."

"A woman, you think?" Conway nodded once and then put that thought aside. "I've gotten the manpower assessed with Sergeant Cohen here, Fitz. It doesn't work out worth a damn. I'm afraid I'll need you, Matt, and Mr. Taylor."

"You're going to command the detachment personally, sir?" Fitzgerald asked, registering mild surprise.

"Regiment requested it, I'll comply. We'll leave a bare-bones force here at Number Nine. After all, we've got between three and four hundred Indians to escort, and if experience has proven anything to me about these resettlements, it's that there will be a hell of a lot more trouble than Regiment ever anticipates. There are always a certain number of young bucks who change their minds about going along and decide to scatter."

Conway went on, "Sergeant Cohen will remain behind; he can run this post as well as I can." Cohen straightened a little more in his chair in response to the captain's praise. "He'll need Four Eyes. Dutch will stay—it's a tragic sight to see him on a horse, and he's lost outside of his kitchen. Keep Corporal Miller and two or three privates. Anyone wounded?"

"Cantrell's still in bed with that arrow wound," Cohen responded. "MacArthur with the broken leg. Javitts with a burned face and bruised arm. Wheeler with—whatever he's supposed to have."

"Wheeler's a malingerer, he'll ride with us. The other three will have to do for a home guard. You can manage it for three days, can't you, Sergeant Cohen? That's the estimate I'm making, barring complications."

"Can do, sir," Cohen said confidently. Conway nodded. He knew damn well Cohen could handle it. Twenty-two years in the army had more than prepared Cohen for any problem that might come up.

"Well and good. Pass the word, collect your gear. Fill up on Dutch's stew. I want to be off by three."

Flora Conway carefully packed her husband's roll and saddlebags as he changed from his dress uniform. She was army, and would never think of complaining about the calls that duty made upon her husband, but she hated to see him go, and he knew it.

When he had finished changing, he walked to where she was carefully wrapping a leftover square of chocolate cake in oiled paper, and put his arms around his loving, generous woman.

"It'll only be three days, four at the most, Flora."

She turned, wearing a brilliant smile. Her fingertips touched his cheek and she bent her head back, offering her mouth to his kiss.

"I know it, Warner. Why, you'd think I was a new army wife, the way you're fretting."

He kissed her again, feeling the weight of her body, the press of her breasts against him.

"Well, it's only that I'll miss you," he said.

"And I'll miss you. In that way I am a new wife, I suppose. I hate it when you're not there to share my bed, Warner. The nights seem so much longer. And colder."

"But you'll get a damned sight more sleep, I'll wager," he laughed.

"Sleep isn't everything," she responded, kissing him again, letting her hands linger on his sturdy, broad shoulders. It was amazing, she thought. Amazing how they still loved one another, how a separation could cause her to go all hollow inside. After all these years—how many of her friends had been so lucky? The smartest thing you ever did, Flora Conway, she told herself, was to boldly ask that young second lieutenant to see you home all those years ago, a lifetime ago in Maryland.

She kissed him again and turned away, chatting too rapidly, packing the cake in his saddlebags.

"To be eaten in a hundred small pieces, or one flattened mess?" he asked dryly.

"You enjoyed it so much, Warner," she said with the slightest dismay.

"So I did, dear, but you know it's foolishness to pack something like that."

And she did, of course, but it seemed a small, important gesture. A little touch of loving remembrance, a small thoughtfulness. Something to enjoy on the long trail, something to remind him of home. Warner seemed to see some of those thoughts in her eyes and he shrugged and said gruffly, "Maybe it will make it to night camp if I'm careful."

Inexplicably she threw herself into his arms and he held her tightly, slightly embarrassed by this sudden show of stark emotion. A knock at the door extricated him.

Flora stood back, smoothing her skirt, and Conway called, "Come in."

Lieutenant Taylor opened the door, nodded to Flora, and reported, "Just about ready, sir."

"Fine. Be with you shortly."

Taylor nodded and disappeared with a faint smile. Flora kissed her husband once more and walked him to the door, carrying his saddlebags for him.

Private Malone staggered into the sunlight, clawing the sleep from his eyes. He had eaten and lain down for what seemed to be only minutes of blissful sleep. Then they were shaking him from his sleep. Men were grumbling, moving around like automatons.

"Duty calls," Wojensky had said with a grin.

"Fuck duty, I need some sleep," Malone had grumbled, trying to roll over and shake Corporal Wojensky's hand away.

"We're moving out."

"I just came off duty!" Malone said angrily, sitting up.

Wojensky had backed off a step. He had seen Malone come out of his bunk like a wildcat before. He shook his head as if with great sadness.

"You're on a bad roll, Malone, sorry. We're riding out—and that includes everybody but the wounded."

"Lend me your gun and I'll shoot myself in the foot," Malone growled. Slowly he came to his feet, grumbled, "Chrissakes," and began searching fuzzily for his boots.

Private Wolfgang Holzer was nearby, dressed crisply, an insufferable smile on his lips. Malone barked at him, "Christ, Holzer, don't you have enough sense to at least not *look* so goddamned pleased about it?"

"Good day," the German answered. He bowed and, still smiling, repeated, "Good day, Malone."

"Christ," Malone breathed. Someday he would find that recruiting officer who had roped Holzer into the army and break his goddamned neck for him. Fresh off the boat, unable to speak a word of English, Holzer had eagerly signed the recruiter's papers, not knowing what they were, not discovering that he was in the army until they had him dressed and shorn. Maybe Wolfie thought the military was compulsory in America; maybe things had been so bad where he came from that he welcomed the clean bed and ample grub, but Malone had yet to see the man unhappy with his condition. He did his job eagerly and was a damned fine soldier, once he understood what he was supposed to do. It was the understanding gave have him trouble.

"We're all going out to fight the biggest goddamn Sioux uprising in five years, Wolfie," Malone said, buttoning his shirt. "Probably all get killed and lose our hair."

"Yes. Good day, Malone," Holzer answered, snapping his heels together. He picked up his blanket roll and followed the others toward the door as Malone stood watching, shaking his head.

"Come on, Malone!" Wojensky called. "Don't want to get left behind."

Malone looked to the heavens and closed his eyes tightly. Muttering curses, he snatched up his blanket roll and canteens and followed. Wheeler was hanging back in the shadows, still trying to find some way out of this detail, and Malone barked a laugh.

"Got you on your feet, did they!"

The narrow Kentuckian turned morose eyes to Malone. "You oughtn't to laugh, Malone. My gut's killing me. I dunno what it is."

"You don't! It's all that damned bellyachin', Wheeler. You're starting to believe yourself."

"If I could only find a doctor who knew something. If I could get East, I mean . . ." Wheeler followed Malone out of the barracks, his words trailing away as Malone deliberately angled away from him.

In half an hour they were saddled and formed up. Captain Conway stood on the plankwalk for a minute, studying them. They saw him turn and say something to his wife and to Sergeant Cohen, who stood with her and Maggie Cohen. Then Conway walked to his horse and signaled to Fitzgerald, Taylor, and Kincaid, and led out at a walk.

The three lieutenants in turn led their platoons out of Outpost Number Nine, trailing dust behind them that sifted through the clear sunlight and slowly settled, leaving the outpost strangely empty.

Corporal Miller and a dismal-looking Herman Javitts swung the gates shut, and then there was simply nothing left to do. Smoke rose from the kitchen, but there would be no one to eat Dutch's cooking this night. The sutler, Pop Evans, lounged in the door of his store, knowing he would have an empty till that evening.

"I've work to do," Cohen said, touching his hat to the two ladies. He was gone then, his boots shaking the plankwalk, and Maggie Cohen turned to Flora Conway, who still watched the distant funnel of dust.

"This will give us a chance to change those curtains, won't it?" Maggie asked the captain's wife. Flora turned to her with a grateful smile.

"It will," she said, slipping a hand around Maggie's waist. "Warner can't complain about it until it's too late. He'll have those rose-pattern curtains on the windows when he gets back, and he'll just have to like them." She laughed, but it was an unconvincing laugh. The two women went into the captain's quarters, and again Flora was grateful for Maggie Cohen's company. They would have coffee and discuss the curtains, laugh and chatter and everything would be fine.

Until evening, when she would have to face that empty bed.

The detachment rode northward at a brisk pace. The wind was cold across the plains, bending the long grass before it. Windy Mandalian rode the point, liking the feel of the wind, the long sweep of the plains, and the distant mountains, appearing as low, dark mounds against the horizon. That was the Bighorn Range, and they would shake free of the horizon and grow larger before the column reached the Powder River. Windy meant to follow the Powder northward to Montana Territory. There should be no trouble with the Indians. They were a large party, and since Crow Foot had been run down two years back, Windy hadn't heard a whisper of any hostile activity in the area.

He settled back in the saddle, letting the wild wind buffet him, taking deep, heady breaths. Conway was enjoying the ride almost as much as his scout was. The wild land around them was untamed, free. A mile off, toward the Bighorns, a small herd of buffalo grazed placidly. Earlier they had seen a magnificent bull elk with

26

his harem of does, lifting their heads to watch them pass, hardly frightened—perhaps they had never seen men before: It was still possible.

Malone didn't share the intoxication. He was uncomfortable perched on that McClellan, and had had little sleep, little to eat. He kept up his usual stream of grumbling against the army as he rode. McBride, watching him, smiled. If there was ever a man who loved the army so much and cursed it so fulsomely as Malone, Reb hadn't met him.

The man was a brawler, a drinker, and a damn fine soldier. There were plenty of men who couldn't take Malone, but Reb wasn't one of them. They were close; Reb had even seen Malone during those rare moments when some of the crust fell away from him.

McBride tilted back his hat, began whistling to irritate Malone, and looked around at the long grass and scattered cottonwoods. The High Plains had Texas beat all to hell, he decided, and it was tough for a Texan to admit that there was anyplace on God's earth that was better than Texas.

Beside and slightly behind Reb rode Wolfgang Holzer, his face shining with enjoyment. The man was amazing. Next to Holzer rode Ned Wheeler, leaning slightly forward, rubbing his stomach so that everyone would know he was sick. Maybe he was hoping they might still send him back to Number Nine, but it wouldn't work. Wheeler had been playing that game until it was worn out.

Wheeler had had that bellyache for six months, ever since the day he got a letter from his girl back home. A whining, wheedling letter—Ned Wheeler had showed it to Malone—saying she couldn't stand it with him in the army, and if he couldn't get out, she was going to marry a freighter she had been going out with. So the mysterious ailment had begun.

Reb looked away from Wheeler and studied the long distances ahead of him. He shifted in his saddle, won-

27

dering again how a soldier like McClellan could have devised such an instrument of torture, and settled in for the long ride.

From the grove of broken cottonwoods on the low knoll to the east, eyes watched as Easy Company trailed northward. The mind behind the eyes counted the soldiers and speculated.

When the last of the blue column had disappeared into the distances, Hal Blodgett risked shifting his position. He shifted his bloodied arm, winced with pain, cursed the army for the hundredth time in an hour, took a deep drink from his canteen, and lay back uncomfortably.

The army, the way Blodgett figured it, had cost him a month's wages when they chased him off that wagon train. More than that, they had cost him a good crew. Sam Donnel, Marty Grubb, Art Sanders — all dead. Then there had been that tall sulky girl. . . . Blodgett had meant to try her on for size. His arm was bothering him. His shirt sleeve was stiff with blood.

He had to have it seen to, and he had an idea. The renegade Arapaho, Pipe, was holed up not far from here, with three or four of his people. Blodgett only half trusted Pipe, but the Indian had nothing to gain by killing him, and Blodgett had done the man a favor a time or two.

He struggled to his feet with the help of the tree, and hobbled toward his horse. He was halfway there before the notion struck him.

A slow, dirty grin spread across Blodgett's wide mouth, and he turned slowly, looking northward to where the mounted infantry had disappeared over the horizon. Then, with a slow nod, Blodgett hauled himself up into the saddle and turned his big gray southward.

three ⎯⎯⎯⎯⎯⎯⎯⎯

They met them on the Powder River, not a hundred miles east of the Little Bighorn: trail-dusty cavalry from out of Fort Keogh, slowly, almost gently herding their human charges south. Two hundred and eighty Northern Cheyenne men, women, and children, with their hundreds of horses and dogs.

The lean, dry-eyed major detached himself from the party and rode out to meet them. He and Conway exchanged salutes and introductions. The major, Howard Dennis, had the hard look of an experienced fighting man, which he was. He had been three years on the Northern Plains, and had battled his share of Sioux, Cheyenne, and Shoshone.

"Here they are and welcome to them," Dennis said as Conway, halting his troops, accompanied the major toward the milling Cheyenne.

"Trouble?" Conway asked, his gaze flickering to Dennis.

"Nothing but. Grub's no good, march is too long. Had several breakouts. Sorry to say we had to shoot one buck. Came at my sergeant with a war hatchet. They're sullen now, and it'll get worse."

"Who are their leaders?"

"Two men, Captain. One's an older chief named Dull Knife. He's reasonable, but uncertain. Talks good English. The younger chief is Little Wolf. Keeps a stone face on, doesn't talk much. Some of the men reckon he's whispering war talk. Apparently he wanted to go on fighting. The surrender seems to have been mostly Dull Knife's doing."

The two officers rode among the Cheyenne, who were making camp, setting up their tipi poles, and lighting cookfires. "Takes 'em a good two hours to set up camp and another two to break camp in the morning," Dennis said. "You'll be traveling slow."

Sullen, dark faces turned to watch as the two men rode through the camp. A yellow dog persistently nipped at the heels of Conway's bay horse.

"That's Dull Knife's tipi," Dennis said, nodding. "You might try making friends with him, though I never had any luck."

Dennis removed his hat and wiped back his thin, reddish hair. Conway noticed a long jagged scar running across his crown. A band of white, the red of stitches still evident where no hair grew or ever would.

"Sioux," Dennis said with a bitter smile. He jammed his hat back on his head and said with a sigh, "Well, they're yours, Conway. You might remember one point: their surrender isn't official. The papers won't be signed until they reach Robinson."

"Any chance of you tagging along for a while until we get to know these people?" Conway asked, but Dennis only laughed.

"None at all. I've had enough playing nursemaid, and so have my men. We're bound for Fort Keogh, and I mean right now. I get the feeling I'm pressing my luck with these people, Conway. You take a bit of well-meant advice," he said with a wink. "Watch your butt."

Then, with another ragged salute, Dennis was gone and a whoop went up from his troopers. Conway didn't imagine they loved Fort Keogh so much. With a frown he turned his horse away, wondering just how much trouble Dennis had had—and how much he was letting Easy Company in for.

Captain Conway spotted Windy Mandalian on his heels, talking to a Cheyenne warrior of sixty or so, and he swung his horse that way, the yellow dog still bedeviling his hocks.

Windy was in close conversation with the old man. He glanced up at Conway, but did not interrupt the Cheyenne's words, which came staccato, low and hurried. Finally, Windy nodded, handed a sack of tobacco to the delighted Cheyenne, and stood, walking to Conway's horse, swinging a foot at the dog, which skulked off.

"Eagle Tree," Windy said. "He's my cousin-in-law— or would be, if I was married."

Conway nodded. Windy had lived for a year off and on with a Cheyenne woman named Pale Light. Windy looked worried, and now he told Conway why.

"Did you know about this peace treaty, sir?"

"What about it?"

"That it ain't signed yet."

"That's what Major Dennis told me."

"And might not be." Windy squinted into the dying sun. "Eagle Tree says Little Wolf never did want to make peace, but Dull Knife didn't want no more of his people dying. He agreed to have a look-see at the agency at Robinson, because he's family with the Oglala there. But there ain't been no surrender signed.

"Other thing is," Windy continued, "one of them Fort Keogh soldiers killed a buck named Two Bears for wanting to go off on a buffalo hunt."

"Dennis told me that as well. It makes for an uneasy situation, doesn't it? Fortunately they've agreed to at least have a look at Fort Robinson, and we'll be gone long before they reach the agency. Any problem after that will have to be handled by Colonel Danner."

"You're right, sir," Windy said. "I just thought you might want to know what kind of situation we got here. Little Wolf, he don't hold with none of it. He's convinced the army is going to lock them all up once they get them to Robinson."

"Maybe I can convince him otherwise," Conway said without much hope. Dennis had undoubtedly already tried that; besides, Little Wolf didn't sound like the type who was going to listen to anyone wearing a blue jacket.

The sun was sinking lower toward the upthrust bulk of the Bighorn Mountains. Conway turned his horse away, riding to where Fitzgerald, Taylor, and Kincaid were waiting dismounted.

"I don't want these Indians treated like hostiles," he told his lieutenants, "but let's not get carried away with friendliness either. I get the idea that the tribe is divided. Some of them would still like to make war, and we don't know which are which. We don't have the time to find out, so let's treat them all fairly but firmly—" He smiled. "Sergeant Cohen's theory, isn't it?"

"You don't actually expect trouble, do you, sir?" Taylor asked. Conway shook his head.

"No. But you should be informed that a soldier from Keogh killed a young warrior."

"Shit," Taylor breathed. Conway lifted an eyebrow.

"Exactly, but there's nothing to be done about that now. We've got these people for two hundred miles. Keep your eyes open, stay alert, but remind your men that they are friendlies. Do I have to add, no fraternization?"

"Might be a good way to get a knife in your back," Kincaid said, glancing at the noncoms who clustered around. Wojensky, Olsen, and Wilson nodded in turn.

"I'll make it plain," Gus assured them. "Any man caught playing with the squaws will regret it for a long, long while."

"Fine." Conway shifted his gaze to Kincaid. "Matt, set up the perimeter guard. We'll camp across the river for tonight. Any other problems?"

"A man sick wants to return to Number Nine," Wojensky said with a suppressed grin.

"Wheeler?" Conway asked with disgust. Wojensky nodded. "I've half a mind to send him back—with a note to Sergeant Cohen to place him on company punishment. What's the matter with that man? I thought he had the makings of a top soldier once."

"A woman, sir," Wojensky said with a knowing wink. Conway only shook his head.

"If anything crops up—anything—I want to hear about it right away. Let's keep the lid on this one, gentlemen."

The first guard watch was posted at dusk, as pennants of pale orange and red streaked the vast skies above the plains. Kincaid, who maintained the respect of his men by thoughtfulness such as this, made sure that none of those who had participated in the Blodgett patrol were assigned first watch. They were still short on sleep, as was Kincaid himself.

Trueblood and Holzer sauntered off on foot toward the western perimeter, speaking together, something Kincaid always wondered about. Was it that Trueblood knew German, listened more closely than the rest of them, or simply pretended better?

Malone had already turned in; his snoring was audible for a hundred yards. Dobbs, who was still wearing a patch over his eye, was stretched out beside him, his feet poked out from under the blankets. It was hard to find anything to fit a six-foot-six man, and blankets were no exception. McBride, sleeves rolled up, was tending to the fire.

Kincaid walked back toward the tent he would share with Fitzgerald, watching as Private Rafferty drove in the last peg, checked the lines for tautness, and straightened up.

"It's all yours, Lieutenant," Rafferty told him.

Kincaid thanked him and stood watching the sundown skies for a while. The silver ribbon of the Powder River swept past, separating the two camps. Across the river, smoke rose from a dozen Indian campfires. A coyote called from far out on the plains, and a dog in the Indian camp answered it excitedly. Somewhere a baby was crying.

"Time for a powwow," Captain Conway said, stepping up beside Kincaid. "Want to go along?"

"If you'll give me a minute," Kincaid answered, noting that the senior officer had a fresh shave and had brushed his uniform carefully. The captain gave him permission, and stood meditatively watching the fading skies until Matt returned, then together they started across the river, their horses throwing up dark spurs of water.

Conway had no trouble finding Dull Knife's tipi again, and they dismounted there. Conway rapped on the tent poles, looking around warily for the yellow dog.

After a moment a dark face, that of a middle-aged woman, appeared behind the tent flap. "Captain Conway and—" Before Conway could finish, the woman had disappeared again. She reappeared moments later, and waving a stubby hand, she beckoned the men to enter.

Crouching low, Kincaid followed Warner Conway into the smoky, dim interior of the tipi. Three women sat in the far corner, one nursing a chubby child with flyaway hair. The boy must have been at least two years old, and Kincaid was mildly surprised, but he recalled that Indian mothers weaned their children late—about the time they were old enough to walk up and ask for it. According to Windy, some of them prolonged it deliberately; in many tribes, a nursing mother refrained from sex, another reason some of these Plains Indians practiced polygamy.

The old chief sat before his fire, shirtless, his gray hair hanging down his back. He had been eating, obviously, but he had placed his bowl aside and was now filling a pipe—a good sign, Kincaid figured. Had the old man been harboring a grudge, that pipe wouldn't have made an appearance.

Conway sat down at the old man's invitation, Kincaid to his left. The old man had the pipe started, and the wreaths of smoke—mixed birchbark and tobacco—lay in flat spirals over their heads.

Conway introduced himself and Kincaid.

"Welcome to the house of Dull Knife," the old chief said. His voice was dry and quavering, but his dark eyes were bright, alert.

The skin on the old man's chest hung in folds, his face was crosshatched with lines of weather and age, and he was short a few teeth, but neither Conway nor Kincaid made the mistake of underestimating the man. He had fought many good fights in his day, against the Arapaho, the Shoshone, and the white armies.

Conway took the proffered pipe and took three ceremonial puffs, then handed it to Kincaid, who did the same.

"I have come to speak with you, Dull Knife, to see if there is anything that needs to be understood between us."

"You are the new soldier leader?"

"I am. I understand there was trouble with the other soldiers. I want none with my men."

"No. I do not want trouble, either." The old man had the pipe once more, and he took three long puffs. Nodding with satisfaction, he placed it aside. "A man was killed by a soldier," he said with a heavy sigh, "but it was his own fault. I know this."

"Are there others who do not know it?" Conway inquired. Dull Knife shrugged again before he answered.

"I think so."

"Little Wolf?" Conway persisted.

"Little Wolf does not trust the soldiers," Dull Knife said in a way that left his own opinion open to speculation. "But there will not be trouble over that incident."

A voice from behind Conway interrupted savagely. "No, let them kill all of our young warriors. That is their plan."

Conway turned half around to see a younger Cheyenne

35

standing near the entranceway. His shoulders were broad, his chest deep. He had a scar wandering across his nose and cheek, and wore a silver sun-emblem on a rawhide thong around his neck.

"Little Wolf," Dull Knife said, half as a greeting, half by way of introduction.

"You sit speaking with these soldiers," Little Wolf said, waving a disparaging hand. "What do they want now? Our women?" He stalked forward. "They have our land. They have our blood. They have killed Two Bears!"

"These men are in my tipi, Little Wolf," Dull Knife said, mildly rebuking the young chief.

"And soon they shall throw you out and live in it themselves, if I know the way of the soldiers!" He waved a hand again, started to make another comment, and then, turning sharply, went out of the tipi, leaving the flap open.

"Will you eat?" Dull Knife asked, as if nothing had happened.

"No, thank you." Conway rose. "I only wanted to introduce myself and to say my tent is always open to you. If there is any trouble with my men, any problem, come to me and we will settle it."

Outside, Kincaid took a deep slow breath. Wordlessly, he and Captain Conway mounted their horses and recrossed the river. They were safely on the other side before Kincaid ventured, "Well, I guess it's pretty obvious how things stand. Little Wolf wants no part of us. I imagine he's secretly stirring things up, don't you?"

"Possibly. But Dull Knife seems to have things under control. Matt," Conway said, looking steadily at his lieutenant, "make sure the men understand the situation here, understand it clearly. We'll only be with these Cheyenne three or four days at the most. We should all be able to keep our fists in our pockets and our pants on for that long. I do not want any trouble," he finished, spacing his words out emphatically.

"I'll make sure," Kincaid promised.

He called Sergeant Olsen and Corporals Wojensky and Wilson to his tent within the hour, and again pointedly explained the captain's orders.

"It'll go damned hard on any man breaking the rules," Matt told them, looking from one man to the next. "The captain's dead serious about this. We're on top of a bad situation, men, let's stay on top of it."

"Jesus, was he simmering," Wilson said after they had moved away from Kincaid's tent.

"He was." Wojensky found the half cigar he had been saving and lit it, the match illuminating his face briefly. "And if Kincaid's steaming, you know what the captain's temperature is. Let's lay it out real plain for the boys again. Tonight."

"Think any of them are dumb enough or randy enough to start trouble?" Olsen asked as they walked toward the nearest fire.

Wojensky laughed. "They're all randy enough, but by God, they'd better control it. I'd hate to be the man who steps over the line and gets caught."

Involuntarily he glanced at Malone, asleep on the ground, his fist to his forehead. "If there's anyone who needs special attention," Olsen said, "let's make sure he gets it."

"He's *yours*, Wojensky," Wilson said with a harsh laugh as the three of them stood looking at Malone, so peaceful in his sleep. The scarred, much-broken hands told a different story. "Malone's in your squad."

"Yes," Wojensky said dubiously, "he is, isn't he."

Olsen and Wilson walked away toward their own fires, Wilson still cackling. Wojensky watched them go, his hands on his hips, the stub of his cigar in his teeth.

"What's the matter with me?" Wojensky muttered. "I must be getting soft, letting Willy get to me like that. Hell, Malone's not stupid. He wouldn't start anything." Then Wojensky shrugged it off and began moving around the camp, shaking his sleeping squad awake. When they had gathered, a mass of sleepy-eyed, unhappy men,

Wojensky told them all carefully, firmly what the captain's orders were.

"Chrissakes," McBride grumbled. "You woke us up for that? You already told us."

"I wanted to make sure you understand, Reb," Wojensky said with little patience. "The captain means it." He kept his eyes on Malone as he spoke, but he hardly looked in any condition to start trouble of any kind. Most of his face was hidden behind a huge yawn.

Dismissing them, Wojensky slipped into his own blankets, lying there for a long while with his eyes open, peering at Malone until, disgusted with himself, he rolled over and went to sleep.

At midnight, Reb McBride felt a hand on his shoulder and opened his eyes to the cold night. The stars were bright in a cloudless black sky. Trueblood was hunched over him, his rifle in his hand.

"Your watch, Reb."

"Christ." McBride sat up, feeling stiff and cold. The temperature must have dropped forty degrees since sundown. Rubbing his shoulders, he got to his feet and walked to the fire, where Malone, Dobbs, and Wheeler were hunched close to the flames, drinking steaming coffee.

Still grumbling curses, McBride crouched near them and poured himself a cup. Malone glanced up and said, "Sheep?"

"Sheep," McBride answered. The joke had never been less funny. Even sheep ranchers must be allowed a night's sleep.

"God's sake, Wheeler," Stretch Dobbs growled, "Can't you quit that moanin'? There's nobody around but us."

"It's kickin' up somethin' awful," Wheeler replied. His eyes were soulful, pleading for belief.

"Shit," Malone breathed. He finished his coffee— boiling a minute ago, now cold—and stood and stretched

38

out the kinks and snatched up his rifle.

"Anybody have any trouble the first shift?" Stretch asked.

"Not that they mentioned."

"With my luck they'll have decided to wait till midnight."

"Anybody want to trade posts?" Malone asked.

"Hell no," Stretch squeaked. "I'm stayin' close to the coffee."

Grumbling, stiff from the cold, they broke apart and stood waiting for the firelight to go out of their eyes. Then, when their night vision had adjusted, they wandered off—Malone and Wheeler on horses, the others afoot. Malone surveyed the Cheyenne camp, where all looked silent, and then turned in his saddle to glance back at the army camp. Someone was standing there, hands on hips, watching him, and it looked for all the world like Wojensky, but Malone shrugged that off. What in hell would Wo be doing up when he could bury himself under a nice warm blanket?

Malone's horse splashed onto the shore and he turned its head southward, meaning to keep a good distance between himself and the camp to avoid misunderstandings. He would circle north, meet Wheeler at the midpoint, and then ride back to the river.

Malone buttoned up his greatcoat and settled in for a long night.

Ned Wheeler walked his horse through the quick current of the Powder, emerging just north of the Cheyenne camp. It was a miserable night. Cold and sleepiness pawed at him. Not only that, but his stomach had begun to flare up again. Even worse, this time. Who would believe it? He smiled grimly to himself.

That was something he truly regretted—having pretended he had terrible stomachaches. It had come true: a self-fulfilling prophecy.

He had racked his brains, trying to find some way out

of the army after getting that heartbreaking letter from Elizabeth Ann, and had finally struck upon illness.

For a while it had worked. They had given him bed rest, and when it had apparently persisted, Captain Conway had sent him to Fort Laramie in the ambulance to be examined by the regimental surgeon.

Whatever that doctor had written to the captain, Wheeler had found himself back on the duty rosters because of it. The others had begun to ride him about it; no one liked a slacker when they had to do his work for him. He couldn't blame them.

It was then that he had realized he wasn't going to get out of the army, that Elizabeth Ann was indeed going to marry that slack-jawed, drooling idiot, Tom Farnum. Then the stomachaches had begun in earnest.

They doubled him up at times; it was like having molten metal in your stomach. Try to find someone to believe you now! Instead of sympathy, he only got ridden harder.

The horse exhaled white puffs of steam. The night was bitter. Wheeler cursed himself for having coffee; that had stirred his gut to greater heights of discomfort. "Christ," he muttered, "it must look like Swiss cheese down there."

He tried not to think about it, or about Elizabeth Ann and that grinning ape she was going to marry. He looked toward the Cheyenne camp, found it quiet, and lifted his eyes to the star-spattered night skies.

An owl dipped and darted across the prairie, cutting a dark silhouette, makeng an odd clicking noise in its ruffed throat.

It turned, came back, and swooping low, it darted near enough to Wheeler's head to cause him to shy away violently. "Why, you dirty son of a bitch," he grumbled. He steered away from the cluster of cottonwoods, figuring the owl had its nest nearby and was trying to drive away any intruders.

He looked back across his shoulder and saw the owl

40

flying away, low across the night-frosted grass, and straightened up in the saddle.

At two o'clock he met Malone at the midpoint, and after assuring each other that it was quiet, they turned their horses and walked slowly back toward the river. The night was colder yet, the air biting at Wheeler's lungs. His stomach was in riot.

"I need a drink of water. The colder the better," he decided, and with that in mind he went on past the Cheyenne camp and toward a feeder stream he had noticed earlier.

Slipping from his horse's back, he walked to the stream, holding his fiery guts. He squatted down and cupped a handful of water to his lips. The water was so cold it jarred his teeth on the way down, but it seemed to cool the fire in his stomach some.

He took another drink, and then, standing with a sigh, he saw her.

Wheeler blinked, but it was no apparition. She stood there in the silent night. Young, pretty, smiling warmly. Her slightly heavy hips swelled against the buckskin skirt she wore.

Wheeler took half a step backward, glancing around automatically, but the girl followed him, still smiling. She had a crooked tooth in front, but that did nothing to make the smile less attractive, for it was plainly friendly, vaguely sensuous.

"You are sick," she said.

"What?" Glancing down, Wheeler saw that he still had a hand clamped to his stomach, and he nodded weakly.

"I know medicine," the girl said, taking another step forward.

Wheeler looked around nervously, expecting a brother, a cousin, a father to appear from the night-dark brush. Or, worst of all, a soldier. They had been warned, and warned stiffly, about fraternization.

It wasn't his doing. He had simply come here for a

41

drink. How could anyone blame him? But it must be cut short before there was trouble.

"I have to be going," Wheeler said. The girl still smiled, the starlight glinting on her teeth.

"But you are so sick," she said, approaching him. "I know about medicine. My husband is very old. Very old, and he has very bad stomachaches too."

"I'm sorry to hear that," Wheeler answered, still backing away.

"Yes, you need good medicine."

Wheeler found his back up against a tree suddenly, and the girl, still smiling, approached nearer. Then she was to him and, astonished, he felt the flat of her hand against his thigh.

He swallowed twice, started to move away, and then stood stock still. Deftly, before he could object, she had undone his trousers, and now stood there cradling his penis in her palm. Slowly her fingers encircled it, and she leaned nearer as she let her hand slide to its base and then slowly back to the sensitive head of it. Wheeler's legs began trembling. *My God, if I get caught!* he thought. But what could he do about it?

She still had him pressed against the trees, and now her hand slid back and forth along his pulsing, increasing erection with more urgency; her eyes were bright, and she made small kittenish noises.

Her other hand dipped between his legs and hefted his sack, and Wheeler saw lights flashing behind his eyes. He closed his eyes. *It's a dream,* he tried to convince himself. But the gentle stroking of the fingers, the soft press of her body against his was real, too real.

Then the hands fell away. Wheeler's eyes blinked open. He started to move, but she grabbed his upthrust shaft again. "Don't run away," she said teasingly.

Then, releasing him again, she removed her dress with amazing sureness. Her hand had recaptured him before he had time to move, and again she pressed against him, only this time she was naked in the night, her breasts soft against him, her thigh against his.

"If we get caught—" Wheeler began, but his protest was feeble. If there was a man alive soldier enough to walk away now, Wheeler had never met him. He surrendered, closing his eyes.

He put his arms around her, feeling the smooth tapering of her back, the sweeping swell of her strong, muscular hips. Her arms went around his neck, and in one quick motion she lifted herself and settled the head of his shaft against her warmth, snuggling closer to him, letting him slide into her depths.

She clung to him, her legs around his hips, her arm around his neck, swallowing him. He kissed her mouth, finding it supple and eager, and forgot everything—the warnings, the cold of the night, Elizabeth Ann.

"You see, good medicine," she breathed as her hips thrust against him, moving in tormenting, compelling circles. She was hot and moist, and Wheeler let out a long slow moan.

He shuddered and she felt it. Smiling, she kissed his mouth again and still more emphatically buffeted his pelvis with her own, her motion silky and rhythmic.

He felt his climax rising, felt a hot sensation speed along his spine and burst inside his brain, felt his loins begin to tremble spasmodically. He clamped the quivering, rubbery moons of her buttocks in his hands and pressed her against him, driving in deeply, answering thrust for thrust as she laughed throatily, whispering, "Yes, yes, yes..." until the motion, the sound of her satisfied voice, the undulating of her fevered body brought him to a high, hard climax and he staggered, nearly falling, as his brain filled with bright lights and his legs went limp.

She laughed again, biting his ear, her legs still wrapped tightly around his waist, her scent mingling with his in the night.

43

It was insane, but he did not want to stop now, did not care for safety—let them shoot him! He lay her down on the cold earth and she accepted it willingly. For a few minutes he was still, stroking her full breasts in amazement, kissing her slender throat, and then he began again, the need surging up.

The woman rocked beneath him, swaying from side to side, a soft murmuring in her throat. A pleasant, satisfied sound, it was somehow exciting to Wheeler. He hovered over her, slowly driving into her body, then slowly withdrawing until need quickened his thrusts and his body collided with hers and they struggled almost like adversaries in a combat of lovemaking.

He felt the woman tense, felt her hands claw at his shoulders and back. She grunted as she grasped for him, her fingers making tiny, urgent motions until he responded by falling against her, pressing tightly against her, reaching sudden fulfillment.

They lay there on the dewy grass, their breath steaming out of their nostrils. She gave him warmth against the coldness of the night, and Wheeler stayed with her, knowing it was dangerous, but not caring.

She pulsed against him, now and then quivering with delight. He stroked her firm thighs, kissed her breasts, taking the tender buds of her nipples into his mouth, kissed her full, parted lips, and sighed, snuggling against her until at last she wriggled unexpectedly, urgently.

"What is it?" He asked sleepily. Following her pointing finger, he too saw the gray light in the eastern skies. "I don't want the dawn to come," he said, kissing her throat, smelling the spice of the woman's flesh.

"Again, tonight," she said demandingly, and he nodded agreement.

"If I can."

"You must." Her eyes searched his, and he nodded again.

They rose stiffly. Wheeler's legs were stiff with the cold. He watched the woman dress, then she came to

44

him, and as the first gleam of dawning silvered the sky, she kissed him again and slipped away.

Wheeler stood watching her for a long moment, and then she was gone, the willow brush swallowing her up. It was only then that the enormity of what he had done hit him.

Disobeying the most explicit order, he had made love to a Cheyenne woman. Only a fool's luck had kept him from being discovered. Staggered by the sudden realization, he walked to his horse, which eyed him soulfully.

"I'm a damned fool, horse," Wheeler said. He promised himself that he would have nothing to do with her again. Why press his luck? It was done and he had gotten away with it. But tonight? Never!

Having satisfied his sense of obligation, he swung into the saddle—and it hit him. The stomachaches! Gone, completely gone. Not a stirring for hours, no pain, no fiery discomfort. Wondering, he touched his stomach and turned his bay toward the camp across the river.

He couldn't help it, he was grinning. A wide, self-satisfied grin split his lips and he began to whistle.

Malone was at the river crossing, and he was scowling heavily. Wheeler tried to erase the grin from his face. Doing his best to appear casual, he walked his horse to where Malone waited impatiently.

"Goddammit, it's about time! I was ready to turn in the report."

"Report?"

"You missed two rendezvous. Dammit, I thought you'd gotten yourself scalped."

"Sorry," Wheeler said. *Damn,* he was still grinning, and Malone was fuming.

"Where the hell were you, anyway?"

"I must've gotten my times mixed up. I was there at the rendezvous. I waited for you. I was thinking *you* had gotten in trouble," he lied fluently.

"Wheeler, I— Goddamn, you're smiling!" Malone had never seen Ned Wheeler break a smile before, not in six months. Malone's eyes narrowed. "Now what in hell . . . Ned?"

"Nothin' at all, Malone. Everything's fine." Then he waved and walked his horse into the river, leaving Malone to speculate.

Malone watched as Wheeler crossed the river, whistling, and clambered out on the far bank. He watched a moment longer, then started his own horse across. Then it came to him. Remembering the sly grin, the faint musky scent about Ned Wheeler, he stopped his horse in the current and looked toward the camp, where Wheeler was walking his horse. "The son of a bitch!" Malone breathed softly. "I'll be damned all to hell if he hasn't had a piece of ass."

He knew he was right as soon as the thought entered his mind, and he shook his head in wonder—wonder at the change in Wheeler, at his good fortune, at his disregard of the captain's orders.

Tell you one thing, Ned, he said to himself, *you're lucky it was me ridin' guard with you.* He started his horse forward and suddenly found himself grinning as well. He laughed out loud and repeated, "The son of a bitch!"

Breakfast was beans and salt pork augmented by pan bread—Rafferty's welcome contribution—and gallons of coffee. Already they were missing Dutch Rothausen, a sentiment hard to support when they thought of the red-faced bully of a cook. But no one had ever said Dutch could not cook.

The soldiers were packed and ready to roll out hours before the Cheyenne had struck their tipis, had their leisurely breakfast, washed in the river, and decided all the omens were favorable for another day's trek.

The men of Easy Company waited with shortening tempers, the sun hot on their backs as it rose higher, their butts sore from the saddle, their backs stiff from sleeping on the ground.

Finally, Conway—looking as cool as if he were on

a spring picnic—nodded to his officers, and the patrols were organized: Mandalian to the point with McBride; two squads under Fitzgerald and Kincaid at the flanks; and the third squad, under Mr. Taylor, at the drag.

They moved across the river slowly, moving no faster than the pace of the slowest walker among them, their faces impassive. Now and then a hostile glance would focus on one of the soldiers—a glance returned, ignored, or answered with a smile, depending upon the man.

The last of their Cheyenne wards was just splashing up out of the river when Conway heard a shrill, pain-inspired yapping. Turning in his saddle, he saw a yellow dog—the same troublesome one?—pawing frantically at the ground, its jaws wide in suffering. A Cheyenne pony had apparently kicked it, something Conway could understand if it was indeed the dog which had harried his own horse. Unperturbed, the Cheyenne rode on, except for one small, dirty boy who was kneeling pathetically by the dog, trying to calm it, though with little success. He looked up pleadingly to the passing warriors, the uninterested Easy Company men, finding no one to help until Wolfgang Holzer halted his horse, stepped down, and walked to the boy.

As Conway watched, Holzer examined the dog; then, after a primitive sign-language conversation, he hefted the large dog, somehow got the animal over the withers of his horse, and stepped up behind it, stroking the dog as the boy watched.

The boy suddenly grinned, and Holzer grinned in response. Somehow they had found a channel of communication, this German soldier and the young Cheyenne boy.

"Want me to talk to Holzer, sir?" Corporal Wilson asked.

"Why?" Conway responded.

"Sir, he can't carry that dog all the way to night camp."

"He can," Conway disagreed. "And I think we'd better

let him if he wants to. Even if the owner is only a small Cheyenne boy, I think we can use all the friends we can make on this journey."

Wilson shrugged, saluted, and started his own horse forward. With a glance toward Holzer, Captain Conway did the same, following the colorful, dusty parade southward.

four ───────────────

They had their first trouble at nooning. It was Rafferty who was involved: Rafferty, quick to smile and slow to anger, and a hot-blooded follower of Little Wolf named Mountain Star.

The morning had been hotter than the previous day, and Conway had held back on the noon halt until they had found water. After first caring for their horses, Easy Company lunched on the same beans and salt pork that they had had that morning.

But Rafferty had never gotten to his meal. Leading his horse to the stream, he stood in the shade of a huge old sycamore, watching it drink. A meadowlark sang in the distance, and among the moss-spattered granite boulders clustered around the shady spot, a pair of playful squirrels chattered and chased one another. Rafferty watched them for a time, deciding there just might be bass in the stream where it had carved out a deep sink in the shade of the rocks.

He heard his horse whinny and looked around to see Mountain Star leading his paint pony to water. The Indian was bare-chested, wearing leggings, moccasins, and a necklace of red beads. He had his totem feathers knotted into his sleek black hair.

The Cheyenne noticed Rafferty, gave him a contemptuous glance, and got down to drink beside his horse. Rafferty sauntered over.

Mountain Star got to his feet, wiping the water from his chin. He was tall for a Cheyenne, a head taller than Rafferty, and heavily muscled.

He nodded. "Fine horse."

"Thanks," Rafferty answered with a smile.

"You give him to me?"

Rafferty laughed out loud and shook his head. "No. He's the only one I got, and the army don't take kindly to soldiers giving their horses away."

He took the saddle from his bay's back and rubbed it down. Mountain Star's eyes were on him the whole time. Rafferty looked across the bay's back and smiled, but the Cheyenne was not smiling back.

"You give me horse, soldier," he said more sharply, and Rafferty recognized the game for what it was. Men played it the world over. Back in the hills of Tennessee, Rafferty's home country, they tried to bully flatlanders out of tobacco and change. In any saloon, you could find men playing the game. Bully the stranger, see if he'll be scared enough to give you what you ask for. Usually it was a group sport, but Mountain Star had the hang of playing it solo.

He slipped his knife from his sheath and stood turning it, the sunlight glinting off the blade. "I have killed many soldiers, many," the Cheyenne said menacingly.

"Have you?" Rafferty shrugged. Maybe it was that boyish face of Rafferty's, his small stature, but the Indian wasn't backing off. He came forward three strides, his eyes haughty, the knife still in his hands.

"You scared of me, soldier man?"

"No." Rafferty turned away and began examining the hoof of his horse. There were two things not to do—run or fight. Rafferty was walking the fine line between these options.

The Cheyenne pressed it. "Maybe I fight you, huh? Take your hair, soldier." He was so near to Rafferty that the soldier could smell the slightly acrid odor of his breath.

"Maybe." Rafferty straightened up. "But not here, not now, not for sport."

Rafferty turned away deliberately, picking up his saddle. Before he could turn back, he heard Mountain Star's yell, saw him flash through the air. Then he was on Rafferty's horse. Heeling it roughly, he jumped it into the river. With a wild, playful scream he was gone, his head thrown back in laughter, riding Rafferty's horse hell-for-leather up the creek.

Rafferty shook his head slowly, turned, and threw his saddle on the Indian's war pony. Mounting, he turned and rode the paint back toward the camp, drawing amazed glances.

"Rafferty!" Sergeant Olsen shouted, waving an excited arm. "What in hell are you doing riding that Indian pony?"

"Traded for him, Sarge," Rafferty said with a grin. In the distance he could still hear Mountain Star screeching. Lieutenant Fitzgerald was striding over to where Olsen and Rafferty were talking.

"What's happening here, Rafferty?" Fitz demanded.

"I'll tell you, sir. An Indian favored my horse, asked me to give it to him, and I refused, it being government property and all. Well, that didn't satisfy him, so he waved a knife and stole my bay. I didn't want to start trouble, calling him a thief and all, so I figured maybe it was a trade. Being as I can't go around dismounted, I saddled up his war pony and rode it back."

"What in hell are you trying to pull?" Olsen wanted to know.

"Nothin'. I'm tellin' it straight, Sarge. What should I have done? Got into a brawl with him?"

"Rafferty's right, Sergeant," Fitzgerald put in. A small crowd of soldiers had gathered around now. "If the Indian took his horse, Rafferty was right to assume it was a trade rather than theft. Talk to Quinn, Private Rafferty. Trade this paint for one of his packhorses."

"Hell, I was just gettin' kind of attached to him, sir,"

51

Rafferty said. At Fitzgerald's flat, hard look he saluted. "Yes, sir."

"Makin' a spectacle of himself," Olsen muttered. "He just wanted an excuse to show up on an Indian war pony. Too many goddamned jokers in this outfit. If it was up to me—"

"Look out!"

Trueblood's shouted warning came just in time. Olsen leaped aside as the Cheyenne on the army horse pounded through the camp, scattering men and horses, his eyes fixed wrathfully on Rafferty.

Trueblood turned, holding his holster down, and raced after them, Malone and Olsen on his heels. They were too late. Mountain Star threw himself from his horse and slammed into Rafferty's back.

Both men hit the ground jarringly, the horses shying away violently, and Mountain Star was first to his feet. He produced that long-bladed knife, and before anyone could reach him he dove at Rafferty, who still sat, dazed, on the ground.

Dazed Rafferty was, but he was alert enough to go down on his back and kick out hard with both legs. He caught the diving Cheyenne in the ribs and flipped him over his head.

Rafferty spun and got to his feet, and Mountain Star, screaming a savage curse, rose also, knife held low. He never saw the pistol in Malone's hand. Malone cracked down hard, catching the Cheyenne flush on the skull, and the man fell like a sandbag, lying motionless against the earth.

"Thanks, Malone," Rafferty said, spitting out a mouthful of blood.

"Don't mention it—until payday," Malone said with a grin.

Captain Conway was elbowing his way through the crowd. He was furious, and Malone braced himself. *It had to be me*, he thought.

"What in the bloody hell is this?" Conway demanded at the top of his lungs.

"It's what you might call an incident, sir," Malone said, coming to rigid attention. Rafferty, blood trickling down his chin, was also at attention.

Fitzgerald spoke up swiftly. "I saw most of it, sir. A game that got out of hand. Malone's responsible for none of it but saving Rafferty's hide." The lieutenant stooped and picked up Mountain Star's knife.

Now some of the Cheyenne were beginning to gather around them, and Conway saw Little Wolf strolling, stone-faced, toward them.

"Better tell me about it fast," Conway said, nodding toward the approaching Cheyenne chief, and Fitzgerald did. Mountain Star was on his knees, holding his head and moaning, when Fitzgerald was finished.

They heard the angry muttering of Cheyenne voices, and turned to see Little Wolf. He threw off his blanket and raged, "What is this! Who has done this?"

Malone was tempted to own up to it, but he kept his mouth shut for once. Little Wolf circled Conway, who was tight-jawed.

"You are so different than the soldiers from Fort Keogh," Little Wolf said with heavy sarcasm. "You are our friend. You have beaten one of my people."

"He stole an army horse," Conway said, his voice remarkably controlled. "And we let him keep it, taking his war pony as trade. Then he came back and assaulted the man whose horse he had stolen."

Little Wolf spat contemptuously, within inches of Conway's boots. The old man looked down slowly and then back up into Little Wolf's face, and Fitzgerald thought he had never seen the captain so near the breaking point as he looked just then. But Conway had remarkable control; a single deep breath and he relaxed again, calling upon all his self-discipline.

Little Wolf turned away angrily and spoke to Mountain Star, who looked up dismally, still holding his head. Little Wolf launched into a tirade, turning to look at the Indians who were watching. Then again he spoke to Mountain Star, more harshly it seemed, and the warrior got to his feet and stumbled away, Little Wolf following him.

"Well," Conway said after they had gone, "that was close enough, gentlemen. I don't want it any closer."

"Can't blame our people, sir," Fitzgerald commented.

"Damn it, Fitz, I don't blame them! I just don't want any more incidents of any kind."

"No, sir," Fitzgerald replied. His eyes followed Little Wolf as he stalked back toward his camp. "The thing is, I don't see how we can avoid them if the Cheyenne *do* want incidents."

Conway didn't answer. He too watched Little Wolf haranguing his people, and he shook his head, thanking God they had only another two days of this. There was a slow fuse sputtering away inside of the Cheyenne war chief, and if someone didn't put it out, there never would be a signed surrender.

Dusk found them only thirty miles south, camped along the crumbling bluffs that lined this section of the Powder River.

Matt Kincaid walked among the men as they sat over coffee after eating. Their faces were grave now, in sharp contrast to the cheerfulness of two days ago. Kincaid saw only one man smiling—Wolfgang Holzer, who sat with a big yellow dog at his feet and a small, bright-eyed kid beside him on a tent pack.

Holzer was making shadow figures with his hands. The flickering firelight cast shadows that delighted the Indian boy; as Holzer arranged and rearranged his fingers, a horse, a dog, and a bird appeared in sequence against the tent behind them.

At Kincaid's approach, Holzer came smartly to his feet and clicked his heels. The kid exactly mimicked

Holzer, even to slapping his bare heels together. Kincaid smiled and shook his head.

"Good night, sir," Holzer said.

"Good evening, Holzer." Kincaid looked at the kid. The firelight shone in his dark button eyes. His face was dirty, his hair hanging in his eyes.

"Maybe the boy ought to go over to his own camp, Holzer. There might be trouble." As he spoke, Kincaid pointed at the boy and then flagged a thumb toward the Cheyenne camp. Holzer nodded reluctantly.

The boy too got the message and he nodded, if a little sullenly. Turning, he saluted Holzer, who quite soberly saluted in return. Then the boy, patting the dog to get its attention, turned and ran back toward the Cheyenne camp, the dog loping after him.

The night guard was just going out—doubled now at Conway's order—and Kincaid stood on the bluffs, watching the river laze by. He found himself thinking about Katie Braun. It was ridiculous, and he knew it. He had only talked to her for a matter of minutes, and their conversation had hardly been cordial. Forcing her from his mind, he strode back toward his tent.

In his own tent, Captain Conway's feet were propped up on his cot. He too was thinking of a woman, far away—his wife. He wondered what Flora was doing just now, thought of her pleasant smile, her warm voice, her still-young body. He still could miss her, still could want to rush back into her loving arms. He still loved her, and that pleased him. He worried about her briefly, wondering if she was lonely tonight, and if everything was all right at Number Nine. He shook that worry off. Cohen was there, and Miller. The weather was good. She was sleeping snugly in her bed.

If Conway could have known what was happening forty miles to the south, he would not so easily have cast away his concern.

The dark-eyed man wearing a fresh bandage that

55

bound his arm to his chest, was drinking whiskey. The renegade Arapaho across the fire from Hal Blodgett had his own jug, and together the two of them were getting slowly, methodically drunk.

"You are sure of this?" Pipe asked again, and again Blodgett nodded.

"I'm sure." With two spread fingers he touched his own eyes. "I saw 'em. There can't be half a dozen men at Number Nine. But there's much loot. Blankets, horses, guns, and women." He had seen the captain's lady once at long range, and even at long range she had looked good.

Pipe made a guttural, indistinct noise as he thought it over, taking another deep drink from the whiskey jug. With each drink, Blodgett's idea sounded better. "I have a cousin—very tame—who lives across the deadline among the Cheyenne. He can see how many men, how many guns."

"Ain't necessary," Blodgett replied. "I know how many men. Don't you believe me?" The liquor was starting to make him lightheaded and quarrelsome.

"I believe. Let us be certain," Pipe said, leaning his hatchet face closer to Blodgett. "Then nothing can go wrong."

"Nothing *will* go wrong. It's a piece of cake, Pipe. A very fancy piece of cake."

"We will see," Pipe answered, leaning back, the fire glossing his bare chest and his sharply featured face. Blodgett was talking through whiskey now, through anger. But his plan was good. If there were so few soldiers at the outpost, it would be almost simple to capture it and loot the army stores. Pipe smiled himself as he thought of the blow to the army's pride.

"I will see my cousin," Pipe promised. He took another long, slow drink, the liquor burning his stomach.

"All right, only don't wait too long, Pipe. I want that fort. I want to cut out a chunk of army hide. They owe me, and Hal Blodgett always collects what's owed him."

The two men drank in silence. Blodgett was in a dark, brooding mood and he drank until his arm was numbed, the fire in it quenched. But the drinking did nothing to cool the hot revenge he planned in his mind. They owed him, and he meant to collect. The loot was secondary. More than anything else, he wanted to humiliate the army. He might even leave his name painted on the stockade wall—that idea appealed to him—or, he thought, I might carve it into the lady's hide.

With that black notion comforting him, he fell into a sound sleep, still clutching his whiskey jug. Pipe managed to stagger back to his lean-to, and after first sending one of his men to talk to his cousin, he too went to sleep, dreaming of his new wealth.

Along the Powder River, the Cheyenne camp slept and the soldiers, on running guard, watched over them. Running guard meant that every man stood watch, in this case for a period of an hour. That kept fresh eyes in the darkness at all times, and assured every man a fair night's sleep.

At midnight, Wheeler was awakened by Dubois, and he crawled shivering from his blankets. He staggered toward the coffeepot, kept going all night now, and was suddenly sharply aware of the night's possibilities.

He had promised himself that he wouldn't meet the girl again. Far too dangerous. But twenty-four hours away from her had sharpened his need, and the risk seemed worth it.

Could he find her? He looked toward the Cheyenne camp, saw a mounted soldier riding slow patrol, and frowned. The odds weren't too good. But there was a chance. He drank his coffee, recalling vividly the clamp of her thighs, the roll and pitch of her thrusting hips, and he felt a slow pulsing begin in his loins.

He saddled his horse and cinched up with trembling hands. Someone, Rafferty maybe, spoke to him, but he didn't answer. He simply swung into the saddle and rode his horse toward the Cheyenne camp, keeping to the brush, the shadows, his eyes searching for her, his ears alert, his impatience growing.

Only an hour, I only have an hour. Damn this running guard!

Half of his time was nearly up already, and not only had he not seen the girl, but he had twice met other sentries—McBride and Dobbs. It began to seem impossible that he could meet the girl and return to camp on time.

And then she was there. Where she came from, he didn't know. She loomed up before him, and Wheeler's heart flip-flopped.

There was no caution in him. He dismounted and followed her nearly at a run to a small depression she had found not a hundred yards from the nearest tipi.

He didn't care. Nothing else mattered. He nearly tore her dress from her and she smiled at his impatience, encouraging him as he sucked at her breasts, his hand diving between her legs to find her soft bush and the damp, warm promise beneath it. He lay her back against the cold grass, unbuckling his belt frantically, and then he was on top of her, the night air cold against his buttocks, his erect sex poised, ready to slip into the warm comfort of her.

There was a smile on her lips as her arms encircled his neck. Then her face washed out with bleak horror.

Wheeler instinctively spun around, and in that instant he had a fleeting, stark view of the Cheyenne's face before he hurled himself through the air, diving at Wheeler. Wheeler rolled aside. Amazingly he wasn't frightened—there was no time to be scared. He reacted instinctively, grabbing for his rifle.

He felt the Indian brush past his body, saw the girl on her knees, cowering, the starlight glossing her body, saw the Indian roll and come to his feet, and Wheeler swung his rifle, swung it with all his might, holding it by the barrel.

The rifle sent a stinging shock through Wheeler's arms as the stock slammed into the Cheyenne's head, and the man went down and stayed down.

"Who is it?"

"My husband—oh, oh!" the girl had her hands to her lips. Her breasts swayed as she trembled and rocked from side to side, her eyes wide. Wheeler bent over the man, touched the warm stickiness in his hair, and put his ear to his chest. He looked up in shock.

"He's dead."

"Oh!" The girl began moaning again and Wheeler slapped her.

"Shut up! You want them to find us? Just shut up."

He looked around in panic, lifting his head above the level of the depression, which he had decided was an old buffalo wallow. No one was around.

"What can we do? They'll find out. They'll cut off my nose and banish me."

"Shut up!" Wheeler hissed. "Get dressed. Help me cover him up."

Nodding obediently, she complied. They caved the banks in over the body, pulling long grass to help complete the job. When they were finished, Wheeler sat back, panting hard. He scattered a little more grass, trying to make the mound of earth look more natural. It was a bad job, but the best he could do under the circumstances.

The girl stood trembling, her teeth chattering together, and he turned on her angrily. "Go on, get out of here. Don't say a word to anyone! To anyone!"

She nodded and scrambled up the bank. Wheeler followed her, checking to see that he had left nothing incriminating on the ground. He stumbled toward his horse, his eyes flashing from place to place. No one. What was that shadow! No, he was safe. He got into the saddle and rode at a rapid walk deep into the willow brush, circled, and reemerged far upstream. It was only then, as he rode toward the camp, that the enormity of what had happened hit him. Maybe they wouldn't find the body, but they would know the man was missing at dawn, when it was time to break camp.

There was no conceivable way that the girl could strike the tipi and ride off with no one noticing her husband was not there. He dismounted and unsaddled as if in a dream. He had killed a man—and possibly had started a war.

Wheeler slipped into his blankets after first tapping Holzer on the shoulder to awaken him. Then he lay with his eyes wide open, watching the stars until morning paled the eastern skies.

five ─────────────

They moved out with the dawn, and Conway breathed a sigh of relief. Somewhere on this day's march they would be met by a force out of Laramie, and Easy Company would be free to return to Outpost Number Nine.

Sitting on a low grassy rise, Conway watched as the Cheyenne strung out southward between his two ranks of soliders. He noticed with faint puzzlement that one tipi had not been struck, and then saw the knot of Indians to the north of last night's camp. Kincaid—or at least it seemed to be Kincaid at this distance—had drifted over there with a dozen soldiers.

Conway kneed his horse and moved that way himself, growing uneasy as he drew nearer. Little Wolf was there, gesticulating wildly, and Kincaid slowly nodded his head. A soldier broke free of the crowd and rode at a gallop to intercept Conway.

It was Wojensky, and he reined in, nearly setting his horse back on his haunches, saluting as he did so. His face was etched with concern.

"They found a Cheyenne dead, sir. Murdered. It's Mountain Star, and they want Rafferty's hide."

Conway didn't answer. Grimly he lifted his horse into a canter and rode toward the tense knot of soldiers and Indians. Now he had spotted Dull Knife among the Cheyenne, and the old chief's face was composed, carefully expressionless. Silently he stood listening to the volatile

61

Little Wolf, nodding from time to time. It didn't look good.

"Conway!" Little Wolf shouted at the captain, but Conway ignored him for the moment.

"What's happened here, Lieutenant Kincaid?"

"A Cheyenne's been murdered, sir. Little Wolf's accusing Rafferty of it."

"Yes, Rafferty!" Little Wolf insisted.

"Dull Knife," Conway said with all the calmness he could muster, "are you certain a soldier did this?"

"What are you saying!" Little Wolf interrupted.

The old chief looked up and nodded. Without expression he pointed out the clearly defined boot tracks surrounding the body. "A soldier did this."

"Then I shall find him. He will be punished."

"You see!" Little Wolf walked around in a circle, slightly hunched forward, arms spread. "They kill us one by one. The Fort Keogh soldiers killed Two Bears. These men have killed Mountain Star. Who is next? You? You?" He jabbed his finger at the gathered warriors.

"The man will be punished!" Conway insisted loudly.

Little Wolf spun to face him. "You must give him to us."

"No. He will be punished, but not by you."

"One of my people has been killed."

"I know this man; he probably brought it on himself. Nevertheless, I promise you his killer shall be found."

"It was Rafferty!"

"Who saw him?" There was no response. "It was a soldier, that's all we know. He will be punished when he is found out."

Conway's eyes settled on Dull Knife, looking for understanding. He found none. The old chief turned wearily away and climbed out of the depression, his eyes going briefly to Little Wolf's. Conway didn't like the looks of this at all. Nodding his head, he rode away, Kincaid at his heels.

Slowing his horse to a walk, Conway asked Matt, "Well?"

"I couldn't learn any more than you did, sir," Kincaid responded. "Apparently one of our men killed the Cheyenne."

"Rafferty?"

"Who knows? We can talk to him, of course, but I really can't believe it was Rafferty."

"Who, then? And why? Do you think Mountain Star jumped one of our people? He was pretty hot yesterday."

"If he did, why didn't the man come and tell us what had happened?"

"That's the question, isn't it? And why there, why in that sinkhole?"

"Only one man knows, sir. And it could have been any of us. Every single trooper was on guard at some time last night."

Conway nodded grimly. There was nothing to do but talk to each and every man—a pointless exercise, really. But someone might have seen or heard something.

"Have Rafferty ride point with Windy, Matt. Let's keep him isolated for a while, until we have time to look into this." He rode silently for a minute, past the long line of Cheyenne with their horses and travois, their yapping dogs and screaming kids. "The hell of it is we're watching as the power in this tribe slips away from Dull Knife and into Little Wolf's hands. You could see it happening back there. Did you see the expression on Dull Knife's face? What was he thinking?"

"Could be wondering if he hasn't made a mistake after all, surrendering, sir," Kincaid commented, echoing Conway's own thoughts.

"Could be. Damn it, it angers me to think we've had a part in this! The detachment from Laramie will be less than pleased, won't they, when I tell them that two Cheyenne have been killed and that there's deep trouble brewing. Trouble that will get worse when we fail to produce the man responsible for killing Mountain Star. I don't think we have a chance in hell of rooting him out."

Neither did Kincaid, but he kept silent. Excusing himself, he rode off to find Rafferty, whom he dispatched to the point. Kincaid told him briefly what was happening, and Rafferty promised to stay clear of the Cheyenne.

"Rafferty!" Kincaid called after him as he had already started forward. "Find Malone and take him to the point as well. Sooner or later someone will remember the part he played in yesterday's action."

"Yes, sir," Rafferty said.

"And Rafferty—at first sight of the Fort Laramie relief, ride back here and report to the captain."

"You can count on that, sir," Rafferty said with a half smile. "There's nobody more eager to get shut of these Cheyenne than I am."

There was, of course, one man who was more eager than Rafferty: Ned Wheeler. Panic pulsed in his head. His stomach had begun to ache in a way that made the old pain seem like a touch of indigestion. How long did he have? They would find out, and he knew it. The Cheyenne would get it out of the girl. Christ, she *had* to be married to that hothead, Mountain Star—her "old, old" husband, Wheeler recalled with bitterness.

He shifted in his saddle, hearing approaching hoofbeats, but it was only Malone and Rafferty making for the point. Rafferty lifted a hand in greeting, but Wheeler did not respond.

I've got to get out of here, he thought. *Might as well be shot for desertion as for murder.* Come dark, he decided suddenly, he would be gone. At least that way he would have a chance. He rode on in sober silence, cursing his fiery guts and his glands.

The day passed with incredible slowness; the yellow sun seemed pasted against the pale skies. Tension was tangible in the air, you could smell it. The Cheyenne were sullen and stiff, the soldiers jumpy, and dusk brought no sign of the relief from Laramie.

Conway was irritable. Summoning Windy to his tent, he told him, "Get down the trail, Windy. Find that relief column and report back."

64

"Yes, sir. You'll be parked here, will ya?"

"No. Our rations are getting damned short. We'll keep it moving toward Robinson. There's every chance you'll run into them tonight, Windy. They can't be very far away. Bring them along if you can. If not, give me their position and we'll angle their way."

When the scout was gone, Conway stood just inside his tent, watching the somber evening skies. Only a single thread of crimson livened the sundown skies. Low gray clouds had settled over the Bighorns, matching Conway's mood with their heavy disposition.

With a sigh he wiped back his hair and called to Fitzgerald, who was nearby: "Start the men in, Fitz."

Fitzgerald waved a hand, and Conway sagged onto his bunk. What a night this would be, interviewing every man jack in Easy Company about the murder. Would he be able to tell a lie from simple nervousness? Would the repetition of questions dull his perception? Probably, he decided, and with little hope he looked up to see Holzer, the first man, standing in the entranceway, grinning like an ape.

Conway sighed and waved a hand. "Come in, Private, I want to ask you a few questions."

It was after midnight before he got the word. Captain Conway was interviewing Stretch Dobbs, who, like the fifty men before him, knew nothing, had seen nothing, when Lieutenant Taylor burst into his tent.

"We've lost a man, sir! Don't know when or how, but Private Wheeler's gone."

There was only a single man on guard duty, and he moved heavily, limping as he walked along the parapet of Outpost Number Nine.

Hal Blodgett watched as the man made one more round, and then he rolled toward Pipe, whispering, "It looks good to me, let's go on in."

Moonrise would not be until near dawn, and with the absence of a moon and the thin sheet of clouds that had drifted over after dark, the night was pitch black, exactly suiting Blodgett's purposes. He watched as Pipe got his four men dispersed, and then, with a nod, Blodgett himself stepped into the saddle and, bold as brass, walked his pony to the gate of the outpost.

He could see the sentry, silhouetted against the dark skies, halt and ready his rifle. Blodgett called out.

"Hallo the gate!"

"Stand still. Who goes there?"

"A message from the captain!" Blodgett replied. The sentry peered down at him, but could make nothing of the face in the darkness.

"Who are you?"

"Sam Franks. I got a place up north. I got a message from your captain."

"Captain who?"

"Conway," Blodgett said with mock exasperation. "Now open up."

"I can't open up for anybody with out the first shirt's say-so."

"Get him, then."

The guard was Private MacArthur, still nursing a tender leg, which had been broken when his horse had rolled on him. He had a bad feeling about this; why would the captain send a civilian messenger?

"What's the message?" he called down.

"God's sake, man, open up. I'm wounded!"

MacArthur hesitated. He should wake up Sergeant Cohen, but Lord, to rouse that bear at midnight was something he had no liking for. But MacArthur wasn't green enough to open the gate on a stranger's word.

"You give me the message or git," he said finally.

He heard the whisper of moccasins on the parapet, half turned, and saw the axe falling. He tried to duck away, but it was too late. The stone head of the axe caught his skull, and MacArthur went down like a pole-axed steer.

Pipe clambered swiftly down the wooden ladder and slipped the gate latch, letting Blodgett in. Then they closed the gate and moved into the shadows. Two of Pipe's men were moving softly across the roof of the outpost, and two others had already slipped to the earth.

Private Cantrell opened an eye and shifted uncomfortably in his bunk. He had been in bed for three weeks, ever since he took the arrow in his chest at Beamon. A man can only sleep so much. Irritably he shifted, trying to find some position of comfort. What had awakened him? He frowned in the darkness of the nearly empty barracks. Lifting his head, he saw Herman Javitts sound asleep. Miller was in his bunk near the door.

It happened again. A trickle of dirt from the sod roof fell through the uneven seam of the planks and rained on his bunk. He gave it no significance and, mumbling a curse, rolled over.

The door to the barracks opened. MacArthur returning already? Cantrell hadn't heard the door, but a cool breeze announced its opening. He turned his head, but saw no one and shrugged mentally.

Then the arms were around him, pinioning him, a body smelling of Indian was pressed against his, and he felt rawhide thongs cut into his wrists. He opened his mouth to shout, and when he did, a filthy rag was shoved in, almost gagging him. He felt his chest wound tear open, felt a rush of dizziness, and sagged back, unresisting.

Miller heard the scrape of a foot against the floor, and came instantly alert. Sizing it up in a single stark moment, he dove for his holstered gun and was clubbed to the floor by an Arapaho.

Herman Javitts fought his way out of deep, troubled sleep. He had been bound up in the frightening web of a nightmare, and now, coming alert, he could not believe he wasn't still dreaming. The face out of the dream hovered over him, mocking, lean, savage.

Hal Blodgett grunted with surprised amusement.

67

"Didn't get all of you, huh?" he snarled. "Maybe I will this time, soldier."

Javitts was rolled from his bunk and tied and gagged. "Wait a minute," Blodgett said. "This boy can help us. Yes, I think we'll use this one. Get up, soldier boy." Blodgett's knife flickered, cutting the rawhide bands around Javitts's ankles.

"How many more men, soldier boy?"

Javitts hesitated; he could see Miller's eyes on him, and Cantrell's. He shook his head, and Hal Blodgett slapped him. His head spun around and his mouth filled with blood. "You don't want your face to look worse than it does, you talk, soldier boy," Blodgett said. He had the soldier by the shirt front now, the muzzle of his cocked Colt shoved up under Javitts's chin.

"Too many for you," Javitts replied with courage that amazed him. Blodgett's hand came around again.

"Don't give me that crap. You want to die, boy? You will if you don't help, I promise you." The pistol barrel jabbed against his throat again. "Tie them together," Blodgett told the Indians. "Quickly. No, not this one. He's my helper, aren't you, soldier boy?"

Herman Javitts felt an anger stirring, an anger like none he had ever known. It slowly spread through his guts and knotted them. He looked into the cold eyes of Hal Blodgett again, seeing the smirk in them, the dark power.

"Move," the outlaw hissed. He shoved Javitts toward the door and out into the cold night. "Where are they, how many? Answer me, or by God I'll kill you here."

"Company clerk—sometimes he sleeps in the orderly room to be close to the telegraph."

"Waste of time tonight. There won't be no messages comin' in," Blodgett said with a humorless laugh.

"First sergeant and his wife. Captain's lady. A man on the gate—"

"He don't count anymore."

There was a pleasure in that statement that revolted

Herman Javitts. He felt like he was going to puke. Blodgett shook him.

"Who else?"

"Rothausen—the cook."

"Who else?"

"Just the sutler. Sometimes the Indian kid who helps him sleeps in the warehouse."

"Who else?"

"That's all!"

"It fuckin' well better be, soldier boy, or you're dead." Blodgett still gripped his nightshirt tightly. Now he shoved him away roughly, turning to Pipe. "Your men know how to hook up a team to a wagon?"

"Not so well."

"Have the soldier boy do it. We'll need a wagon for the loot. When he's through with that chore—do whatever you want." He shoved the rag back into Javitts's mouth.

Pipe smiled every bit as viciously as Blodgett. Speaking in a rapid, low voice, he nodded to the soldier, and one of the Arapahos took Herman Javitts by his bound wrists and propelled him roughly toward the paddock.

From the corner of his eye he could see Blodgett and his renegades creeping across the parade, and he wanted to scream out, fight back, but could do neither. The Arapaho who had hold of his wrists was moving him nearly at a run toward the paddock area. The horses corralled there looked at them curiously, ears pricked. One stocky bay took off at a run around the enclosure.

The Indian moved him ahead and shoved him into the dark, musty interior of the wagon shed.

Javitts looked around in the darkness, his mind racing. He would harness the mules and then he would be killed. Dead. He would be alive for fifteen more minutes, and then he would cease to exist. The Indian prodded him with the rifle barrel.

"Work," he said, freeing his wrists.

Javitts went to the wall where the harness was hung,

and took down a double brace. This he hooked to the yoke, snapping the traces in place as the Indian watched him.

"I can't see," Javitts complained.

"Work."

"I tell you I can't see."

With evident disgust, the Indian allowed him to light one of the coal-oil lanterns. Javitts searched the barn frantically with his eyes. There was a shovel along the near wall; hammers and pry bars hung in leather loops on the wall. The Indian read it in his eyes and smiled thinly.

"I'll get the mules," Javitts said. The Indian went right along with him. The night was cold; Javitts's mind was a blur. Fear rode him mercilessly. Abruptly, across the parade, a woman screamed. Javitts turned around, his eyes wide. The Arapaho was still smiling.

"Woman," he muttered cheerfully.

Woman! It was not just any woman. It was either the cheerful, expansive Mrs. Cohen or the gentle, smiling wife of the captain. Two women who were filled with compassion and love, never rode high-horse over any of the men, indeed went out of their way to be kind. Two outgoing, loving women, friends to all of them. And now that bastard Blodgett—or worse, Pipe—had them. The memory of the tales about Blodgett came back with jarring suddeness. The women killed, raped, battered.

And I let him live!

Herman Javitts stood there suddenly in another man's body. It wasn't his. His own body trembled and was knotted with fear, his eyes were uncertain, his stomach was hollow, half nauseated. This body was different altogether.

He was not angry. He was ice cold, calculating, savage. These men must be killed. The idea came to him suddenly, and he savored it; he wanted to stand over them and batter their brains out, carve them into chunks for the buzzards, set them on fire.

"Work," the Arapaho said.

Herman did so. He looped Old Joe and Gomez, two of their best mules, and led them back to the barn. The mule's hide rippled under his hand as he rested it on Joe's shoulder. The mule was a dignified creature, wily and indomitable. He obeyed commands surely and with alacrity. There was no need for a lash with Old Joe and Gomez.

Javitts had done his time as a muleskinner and he knew how to handle them with a word, the slight pressure of his hand. He backed Gomez into the harness, the Arapaho standing at his back, ready to kill him as soon as his work was completed.

Coolly, Javitts clipped the harness to Gomez, then he half turned, dove back under the mule, and went for the shovel against the wall. The Arapaho shouted, but for some reason did not fire.

Javitts had landed on his belly. Now he stretched out his hand and felt the smooth roundness of the shovel handle, and he saw the Arapaho fighting past Joe, his rifle lowered.

Javitts came to his feet, swung the shovel at the lantern, heard the glass splinter, saw the lamp go out, and hurled himself to one side.

His heart pounding, he lay there clenching the shovel, smelling the straw and mules, the cold metallic slag in the forge. Drawing himself ever so cautiously to his knees, he worked into a crouch and waited.

Adrenaline pumped through him, but he felt no fear. His body was simply priming itself for the task at hand. Javitts still felt as cold as ice, hungry for the Arapaho's death. But the Indian was a ghost in the night.

Then the Arapaho made his mistake. Creeping forward, he silhouetted himself briefly against the open barn doors, and Javitts lunged.

He moved with quickness and savagery he'd never known he possessed. He saw the Arapaho's head come around slowly. Everything was slow; there was time to

71

calculate angles and vectors, to plan for contingencies. Everything was slow but the hammering of his wildly beating heart.

The Indian turned and started to bring his rifle muzzle around, but he was too late, and as Javitts realized he would win, his throat issued a savagely triumphant sound. Not a laugh, but a more primitive, exultant cry. He had the shovel drawn back, and now he drove it forward, using all of his new-found strength.

The shovel buried itself in the Arapaho's guts, nearly cutting him in half. The man collapsed in a rush of blood and gore, a strangled cry dying in his throat, the rifle clattering free. Javitts stood over him, grinding the shovel into him.

He stood there in fascination for a long minute. Who was doing this killing? Who was this man? Surely not Herman Javitts, the preacher's son?

Shaking it off, Javitts picked up the Arapaho's rifle, checked it over—it was a fine new Henry repeater—and slipped out into the darkness.

He wanted to rush toward the captain's quarters. He saw a light there, but caution prevailed and he turned toward the barracks. Had they left a man there? He couldn't recall.

He heard a door opening across the parade, and he pressed himself into the shadows. The sutler's door was open, and an Arapaho stood there, gun in hand, looking around.

Waiting for the wagon, Javitts thought with malicious satisfaction.

After a minute the renegade turned and went back into Pop Evans's store. Javitts moved ahead swiftly, silently. The barracks was dark as he touched the door with his boot toe and slowly opened it.

"Don't shoot," he reminded himself. "Don't shoot if you can help it."

There was no need to. The renegades had left no guard. Cantrell and Miller were coated with sweat from struggling with their rawhide bonds. Cantrell's wound had opened up, and his chest was stained with blood. Their faces came around and passed from surprise to amazement.

Javitts didn't speak. He was to them in a second, untying them.

"Where—?" Miller began.

"One in Pop's place. The rest in the captain's quarters, I think." Javitts and Miller helped Cantrell to his feet, and Javitts gave him the rifle. Cantrell couldn't move well, but he could shoot. Miller and Javitts had the same idea.

"We'll flush 'em, Cantrell. Get in the window. If you see anything crossing the parade, shoot to kill."

"Don't you worry about that," Cantrell said coldly.

They left him in the barracks window and slipped back along the shadowed plankwalk toward the orderly room.

"Wait," Miller whispered, touching his arm.

The corporal gestured toward the kitchen, and Javitts nodded impatiently. As Javitts stood watch, Miller slipped into the kitchen, moving like a cat across the lye-smelling floor.

It didn't take much to find Dutch. He lay there like a trussed buffalo, straining at the rawhide ties around his wrists. Miller touched his finger to his lips before he removed the gag and untied Rothausen.

The man was so mad that Miller could almost feel the heat rising from him. In better light he knew what he would see—a crimson face, bulging eyes, tendons standing taut on the cook's meaty throat.

"They're in the captain's quarters," Miller told Dutch briefly. "Five altogether. Javitts already got one."

Dutch nodded silently, menacingly. He recovered his pistol from under the iron stove where the Arapahos had kicked it, and as an afterthought picked up his seven-pound cleaver.

Miller had seen Dutch go all the way through a haunch

73

of buffalo with that cleaver, bone and all, and he shuddered at the thought of what would happen to a man unlucky enough to get in the way of it.

Reaching the captain's quarters, they heard muffled laughter, an answering moan. Peering over the sill, Miller could make out Sergeant Cohen strapped to a chair, his face a vengeful mask. Opposite him, he could see the bare back of an Arapaho and, facing the Indian, Maggie Cohen with the front of her dress torn away, her ample breasts bobbing free. On her knees, shielding her face with her hands, was Flora Conway.

Cohen relaxed completely and then strained again, working until he was red in the face, until the rawhide cut deep, bloody grooves in his flesh, but he couldn't break loose.

And he wanted to be free, wanted to leap on Hal Blodgett's head and smash him into powder, wanted to tear his throat out for him and trample on him as he bled to death.

"Look at the tits on this one, Pipe," Blodgett said, watching Cohen from the corner of his eye. "Nice big juicy set, ain't they?" His hand reached out and mauled Maggie's breasts, squeezing them until the pain registered in her blue Irish eyes.

Maggie held her head high, however. She looked at Blodgett with the utmost scorn and said, "You're not much of a man, are you?"

"No? You think not?" Blodgett took hold of her breast and twisted it, his face leaning close to hers. "Maybe you'll find out how much of a man I am." He laughed harshly.

"Damn you, Blodgett!"

"Shut up, Cohen. I said I'd let you watch if you were a good soldier boy. Are you going to be good?" Stepping to Ben's chair, Blodgett hooked the leg with his boot and yanked. The chair toppled over, and Cohen's face slammed against the floor.

"You take the one with the big tits, Pipe. Me, I'm

strapping on the captain's lady." He walked back to where Flora Conway sat huddled against the floor, and lifted her chin roughly. "Stand up!" he ordered.

When she did not comply, he bent over, thrust his hand up under her petticoats, and tore her pantaloons away.

"Don't fight it," he said, his filthy eyes glittering. "You might like it. A little raw meat while hubby's away—"

The door burst open. Pipe spun around, but he never raised his weapon. Miller shot him through the face and then through the guts. He fell, a faceless, writhing figure, and Miller vaulted over the dying Arapaho.

From behind the door a second Arapaho lunged, but he hadn't reckoned on Rothausen. The Indian turned toward the door, started to run, and saw the bulk of Dutch Rothausen loom up before him. It was already too late for the renegade. The cleaver caught the lantern light as it descended. It was the last thing the Indian ever saw. The seven-pound cleaver caught him at the base of the neck and, with all of Rothausen's weight behind it, drove cleanly through, neatly decapitating the Arapaho.

His head rolled free, his trunk pumping red blood, as Dutch stepped back to let the body fall onto the plankwalk outside.

At the first sign of trouble, Hal Blodgett had leaped over a tumbled chair and dived headfirst through the window, landing roughly on the plankwalk.

Scrambling to his feet, he began to run. But Javitts had been waiting. He calmly lifted his Schofield, and without calling out, without firing a warning shot, he sighted the bead on Blodgett's white shirt and fired three times. The black-bearded outlaw plowed up the parade with his chin and lay still.

From Pop Evans's store the remaining two Arapahos had emerged, rifles in hand. One bolted, but one hesitated. That hesitation cost him. From the barracks, Cantrell's rifle barked, and as Javitts watched, the Indian was slammed back into the door, arms flung wide, a hole punched through his heart and lungs.

The last renegade made the palisade, but outlining himself against the sky, he made an excellent target. Cantrell, Miller, Javitts, and Rothausen all opened fire and the Arapaho, shot to rags, tumbled over the palisade to the cold earth below.

Javitts still held his pistol, searching for other targets. The smoke drifted across the plankwalk. Someone said something, and it took a moment for the words to reach his brain.

Slowly he lowered his pistol, looking with deep satisfaction on the crumpled form of Hal Blodgett, regretting only that the man had died so quickly.

Miller's hand was on his shoulder, and as Herman lowered his pistol and looked around, the corporal squeezed his shoulder, winked, and said, "You done good, boy. You done good."

six _____

Relief was three days overdue already, and the supply wagon was nearly empty. The Cheyenne were surly and Conway's own men were dragging, irritable. The captain hadn't been able to produce the killer of Mountain Star for Little Wolf, and Wheeler had taken off, pointing the finger of suspicion at himself. Little Wolf had flatly accused Conway of knowing it was Wheeler and letting the man ride off.

The day was dry and dusty. The grass was sparse on the long plateau between the Bighorns to the west and the forbidding Black Hills to the east. Kincaid, with two men, had gone out after meat, and now they were late getting back. It was essential that Matt find game, otherwise the choice would be between letting the Cheyenne go hungry and allowing them to hunt on their own; neither alternative was pleasant to contemplate.

Hour after hour, Conway himself rode point with Rafferty and Malone, squinting into the coppery distances, searching for the relief party. The men riding with the captain were silent, and it was not out of deference to his rank. To talk with dry throats, with the choking dust swirling into nostrils and mouths, was no easy task. Scarfs were reversed and used to cover their faces, but the dust was pervasive. In the rear of the procession it was almost unbearable, and Conway had to move them at a slow walk to make travel possible.

At sundown on the fourth day, Conway made out a narrow, tall figure riding toward them on a leggy Appaloosa pony, and he rode out to meet his scout.

"Where are they?" Conway asked irritably.

Windy could only shake his head. "Ain't comin', sir."

"What did you say?" Conway asked in disbelief.

"Talked to Major Dandridge at Laramie, captain. He says he got no orders to relieve you. Says he's damned sorry, but he can't break loose a detachment on your request. Seems they're having some trouble with the Yampa Shoshone, and he doesn't have the people anyway."

"Damn."

"'Zactly," Windy drawled.

"Well, there's nothing to be done about it. We'll continue on to the Nebraska line and hope like hell nothing's gone wrong with things at that end. Three more days. You didn't see Kincaid out there, did you?" Conway asked.

"No. Neither hide nor hair of no white man, jest a glimpse of a wild Cheyenne."

"Trouble?"

"No. He was skinning an elk. I let him be and he let me be."

Together they rode ahead for another mile, searching for a suitable campsite. They were not far from the North Platte, but too far to reach this evening. It would be a dry camp again, and there would be more grumbling from the Indians.

"They keepin' their war bonnets off?" Windy asked.

"So far, Windy. The incident with Wheeler—I'm still assuming it was Wheeler—damn near brought the thing down on us, but that's quieted a little. Or so it seems. Who knows what they're talking about around the campfires? I only know that Little Wolf is doing a lot of talking."

"Mebbe Eagle Tree has heard," Windy suggested. "I could ask."

"That might be a good idea."

There was little to choose among the campsites on the barren plains, and since the light was failing fast, Conway simply drew up and stepped out of the saddle. He continued to look with some anxiety for Kincaid. They had meat for tonight, but by morning the stew pots would be empty, and there's nothing like empty bellies to stir up anger.

Conway took off his scarf, poured a little water from his canteen onto it, and wiped his face and gritty neck as he watched the long column slowly approach him. The far ranges were swathed in shadow, the high thin clouds were glossed with purple and gold, but Conway was in no mood to enjoy the spectacular scenery.

Kincaid trailed in well after dark. The wagon behind him carried two young buffalo carcasses and that of a bull elk. Conway breathed a sigh of relief and ordered the buffalo taken immediately to the Cheyenne camp where the women could butcher and cook the fresh meat.

"All right to come in, Captain?" Windy asked, peering in the tent.

"Only if you're a whiskey-drinking man," Conway said, and Windy grinned, stepping inside. The captain had a bottle in front of him on a makeshift table, and he shoved the whiskey to Windy, who tossed his battered hat aside and nodded gratefully. The scout took a deep drink, looked with regret at the nearly empty bottle, and started to pass it back.

"You got more, captain?"

"No, but that's all right. Finish it. Did you have a talk with your cousin?"

"I did." Windy stretched out his long, buckskin-clad legs and frowned. "It ain't good, Captain."

Conway waited expectantly as the scout took a chunk of cut-plug tobacco from somewhere deep in his buckskins and wrestled a piece off with his teeth.

"War talk?"

"Not directly, you wouldn't say. But Little Wolf is saying they ought to turn around and go home. Slip away in the night. Dull Knife don't like the idea, but the young bucks say Dull Knife's old and scared. Little Wolf's tellin' 'em the same story—when we get 'em to to Robinson they'll all be locked up or killed. Says the white man is just tryin' to lull 'em to sleep. Then he'll clap irons on 'em. Trouble is, they about half believe him, Captain."

"Does Eagle Tree know anything about the Wheeler incident?"

"Just the same tale. A soldier killed Mountain Star and you let him ride off to hide him. Little Wolf says they all better be ready to fight. Says the soldiers will kill 'em at night, one by one."

"I wish to hell that man hadn't taken off. We may never find out what did happen. Malone told me he thinks Wheeler had a squaw, but he can't say why he thinks that for sure. It's just a notion. Think we could find out?"

Windy shrugged heavily. "Doubt that, Captain. The Cheyenne find out a woman was playing around with one of the soldiers, they wouldn't like it. Not the way feelings are now."

"No. Well, see if you can find out anything, will you?"

"I'll try, sir. But I don't hold out much hope."

Conway walked the scout to the door and they said good night. The captain watched the tall, wiry man amble away toward the fire, heard someone call out in welcome, and saw Windy wave. Then he stood looking over the Cheyenne camp.

He was plain worried, and getting more so. He could beef up the guard even more, but that was taken as a sign of hostility by the Cheyenne, and the more people he posted, the more the Cheyenne worried, perhaps figuring that as they neared Robinson they would be made prisoners.

Conway turned back into his tent, lifted the empty whiskey bottle, turned it before the lamp, and then, sighing, sagged onto his cot, turning the lamp out.

Night guard went smoothly for once, and with dawn the camps were astir, preparing for another long day's trek. The faces Conway saw around his own campfires were drawn and sober.

He couldn't blame them. They had all been geared to returning to Number Nine, sleeping in their own bunks without worrying about the hostile presence, having a dozen or so beers at Pop's, and stuffing themselves with Dutch Rothausen's good cooking. Now all of that would be delayed, and they would ride this moving powder keg for a few more days.

They made good distance that day, and camped along the North Platte that night. Windy brought in a dozen sage hens for the officers' mess. The nights were clear and cold, the days furnace hot.

They moved through scattered timber; cedar in the highlands, occasional cottonwoods in the bottoms. Nearer the river, which they followed for fifty miles, there were willow and bogs, thick with cattails and reeds, alive with frogs, which the Indians and not a few of the soldiers tried gigging, or spearing, with indifferent success.

On the third day, when they had broken away from the river, easing nearer the Nebraska line, the soldiers appeared across the plains, shimmering and bending as the heat screened and distorted them. Still, they were beautiful, and Conway held up the column, watching the men of Fort Robinson riding to meet them.

"Damn," Wojensky said. "Never was so happy to see horse soldiers."

"Ain't they pretty?" Olsen agreed.

Easy Company sat watching their approach. Conway smiled with relief, but the smile faded to puzzlement as the Fort Robinson detachment drew nearer. Lieutenant

81

Fitzgerald was at Conway's side, and it was Fitz who spoke what the captain himself was thinking.

"Damn slender detachment, isn't it, sir? Can that be the main body?"

"It had better not be." Conway's mouth was set grimly. There couldn't have been more than thirty horse soldiers in the party.

Their eyes searched the plains beyond the cavalry, expecting to see more soldiers, but not finding them. Finally the yellowlegs drew up, and their officer, a bleary-eyed, square-faced major, saluted Conway.

"Major Halstead, Fort Robinson."

"Captain Warner Conway, sir. Outpost Number Nine."

"Number Nine? What happened to Laramie?" the major asked, scratching his neck.

"No orders received, apparently. Sir, is this your entire force? As you can see, we've got a large party of Cheyenne here. Truth is, we've been somewhat overworked as it is."

"Trouble?" Halstead asked, ignoring momentarily the first question. He had that slightly superior tone that Conway detected whenever his mounted infantry ran into a cavalry outfit.

"There's been some trouble. Maybe we should dismount and talk about it," Conway said, nodding toward the tempting shade of a nearby cottonwood grove.

"Maybe we should. Sergeant Ritter!" he shouted without turning his head. "Dismount your troopers!"

Stepping from the saddle himself, Major Halstead handed the reins of his horse to a waiting corporal. Then the cavalry officer followed Conway to the nearby shade.

"You might want to sit, sir," Conway said, nodding toward a low-growing, arched limb. "The story may take a while."

Halstead listened attentively to Conway's tale of the trek: the Cheyenne killed by a soldier from Keogh; the later killing of Mountain Star, and Wheeler's disappearance; of the disunity in the tribe; of Little Wolf's apparently growing influence. When he was through, Halstead nodded thoughtfully.

"This is sticky, and getting stickier with each mile, isn't it?"

"I'm afraid so, Major."

"You're right, of course. I hardly have enough men to handle this job. Some screw-up somewhere. The estimate I got was that there were between eighty and a hundred Cheyenne coming in. If I had known what was brewing, I would have asked some of the Oglala to ride out with me and explain that Robinson really isn't a chamber of horrors. I'll try to talk to the old chief myself," Halstead said, rising. "Of course, I shall have to request some of your men to assist us. They already know the ropes and—"

"I beg your pardon, sir, but I need those soldiers as well. They've been out here quite a while, and my own area is sadly underprotected."

"What area isn't?" Halstead asked bluntly. "But you can see my fix, Conway, and I'm asking you for some of your people. I'd hate to put it in the form of an order."

"But you will if necessary?"

"That's about it," Halstead said. The two men rose and stood facing each other in the dense shade. The wind, stirring up dust devils out on the plains, was still warm, although darkness was falling fast. A quail called out along the river. Conway nodded.

"No need to make it an order, then, sir," he replied with a smile. "I'll split my party."

"I appreciate it," Halstead said dryly, as if there had been no coercion. "I'd like at least one officer and a couple of your noncoms as well."

Walking back to where the horses were being held, Conway watched the Cheyenne begin to set up camp again. The cavalry soldiers from Robinson had dismounted and now stood exchanging gibes with some of Conway's men, Malone among them.

Matt Kincaid stood to one side, looking relaxed for the first time in days. Bidding goodbye to Halstead, Conway approached his first lieutenant.

"Everything settled, sir?"

"Everything's settled."

"Pulling out tonight, then?"

"I am. Matt, you're staying."

"Staying?" Matt frowned deeply. Then he half smiled. "A joke, sir?"

"No joke. You can see how undermanned Halstead is. I'm giving you and a dozen men to him on loan. You'll see the party into Robinson, and when Halstead relieves you, come on home."

"All right," Matt replied smoothly. Conway had expected some resistance, and he looked curiously at his lieutenant. You would almost think Matt wanted to go to Robinson.

"Pick your men, then, Matt. I don't suppose it'll make you too popular. They won't relish remaining with the Cheyenne."

"Or with the cavalry," Matt sid mildly.

"The yellowlegs," Captain Conway said with pride, "we can handle."

Kincaid picked his men, and as Conway had foreseen, they weren't happy about it. But they didn't have to be happy. They had to be good, and given the opportunity, Kincaid selected the best, excepting Olsen—Conway wouldn't part with his platoon sergeant.

Holzer accepted it with equanimity. Probably he never had known when he would be returning to Number Nine anyway. He continued to play with the kid and the dog. Malone took it with a soldier's resignation, the same with McBride. Wojensky never argued and he didn't now. Dobbs, Trueblood, Rafferty, and Dubois were among the others chosen.

They made their camp, watching as their comrades

84

packed their rolls and formed up under Olsen and Wilson, preparing to ride out as dusk shaded the western sky.

"See you when you make it, Matt," Taylor said with just a touch of a grin. Fitzgerald was ready to rib him too, but he noticed the odd expression on Kincaid's face, the faint smile, the distant gleam, and he only saluted.

"What's with Matt?" he asked Taylor.

"You saw it too? Funny, he was wearing that same expression when they came in from the Blodgett patrol. I thought then that it was a woman, but I don't know. . . . Maybe the sun's gotten to him. He couldn't have a woman at Robinson, he's never been there as far as I can recall. Not lately, anyway."

"As long as he's happy." Fitz shook his head. "Myself, I couldn't take much more of the Cheyenne. I was having trouble sleeping. Let the yellowlegs have Little Wolf, and luck to them. They may need it."

Fortunately they didn't. The two-day ride to Fort Robinson was slow but trouble-free. The single incident—a young buck took off late one night and was run down by two cavalry soldiers—was resolved without trouble. Yet the faces of the Cheyenne grew grave as Fort Robinson first appeared as a low, dark rectangle on the horizon, then slowly lifted from out of the surrounding plains and became stark and forbidding.

Now, however, the Oglala agency was also in view. The Cheyenne could see the Sioux tribesmen in the fields, where a good crop of corn was growing, or lazing beneath the oak trees, smoking. There was not a soldier to be seen, but only the quiet, neat Oglala camp and the seemingly contented Sioux.

There were small, healthy-looking flocks of sheep and a nice-sized herd of horses, cornfed and sleek. The Cheyenne pointed these out with animation to each other. The Oglala were wealthy, defeated or not. They lived in peace and comfort.

Little Wolf was sullen and dangerously silent; Dull

Knife appeared cautiously optimistic, apparently comforted by what he saw of the Sioux camp.

Matt Kincaid saw little of it. He still had that damned, flashing-eyed girl in his mind, and he had made up his mind to see her, whether she wanted to see him or not.

One of the cavalry officers had brought her name up casually: "Damned lynx-eyed beauty. Won't smile at an army man. Looks right through you, she does. I've given her a try—hell, every man on Robinson has—but no dice. She's a hard one, Kincaid. Beautiful as can be, but solid ice inside, man, solid ice."

Kincaid would see about that. He noticed Wojensky beside him now, and wondered how long he had been there.

"Nice layout they got, isn't it?" the corporal asked.

"One of the best agencies I've seen," Matt had to agree.

"Man, I could live here myself, Lieutenant. Look at that. Herd of horses, patch of land, squaw to keep you warm. Me, I got a rawhide-and-ticking bunk, my boots, and that's it. Money we make, I never will have a patch of land. I ask myself who's winning this damned war sometimes."

Kincaid smiled vaguely and nodded, and Wojensky shrugged. "Riding home tonight, sir, or you going to let the boys have a beer at the sutler's?"

"I think the men could use a beer," Kincaid answered. "I might even join you."

"I'll pass the word, if I may, then. It'll cheer 'em up some."

"Fine," Kincaid agreed absently. The point of the column had already curled to the right and come to a halt a hundred yards from the north wall of Robinson. There the Cheyenne would camp temporarily until the army and the Indian agent could decided how they wanted to arrange things. Probably they would interview the Cheyenne chiefs tonight, and reassure them, and then there would be a slow period of adjustment, but Easy Company's duty was done, and Kincaid had seldom felt more relieved. He felt lucky to have made it this far without serious trouble. The Cheyenne couldn't have forgotten Mountain Star's death, but perhaps they had decided he was asking for it.

Perhaps they too could settle on this green, lovely land and live peacefully, happily. Kincaid hoped so— for everyone's sake.

Stiffly he dismounted, rinsed his face, and watched the hubbub of activity as garrison soldiers came out to relieve the detachment, as the Cheyenne set up camp and their Oglala brothers came to welcome them, as the civilian and military population of Robinson came out to stand and have a look at some real Cheyenne Indians, and Easy Company's enlisted men, freed of their bonds of tension, grappled and laughed and splashed water on each other.

"Kincaid."

Matt turned to find Major Halstead behind him. "Yes, sir?"

"I'm going to report to Colonel Danner. Maybe you'd better come along."

"All right." Matt replaced his hat and dusted his uniform off as well as possible. Then he followed Halstead across the crowded parade ground, where Sioux and white teamsters mingled with trappers and settlers.

"More of a crowd than you're used to, isn't it?" Halstead remarked.

"It is that," Kincaid had to agree.

The orderly room was clean, whitewashed and large. Three clerks sat in a row along one wall. The telegraph key clicked away in the corner. A second lieutenant came to his feet and opened the door for Kincaid and Halstead.

Colonel Danner was a short, red-haired, red-faced man with hands like a bear. He gripped Kincaid's hand strongly, but his expression was hardly warm. He nodded to his subordinate and introduced the spare, white-haired man who sat in the corner.

"Kincaid, this is Lewis Travers, our Indian agent."

Travers offered his hand without rising, and Kincaid shook it, finding it limp and a trifle damp.

"Whiskey?" Danner offered. Halstead accepted, Kincaid declined. The colonel leaned back in his chair, fingers interlaced on his chest. A beautiful, massive Sioux war bonnet hung from the wall behind him. With a sigh he told Matt, "Lieutenant, we're going to need you and your men a while longer."

"Sir?" Kincaid's eyebrow lifted.

"We're awfully shorthanded here, as you can see. And in order to escort these Cheyenne to Fort Reno—"

"Reno!" Kincaid interrupted, obviously annoying Danner, whose red face turned a deeper crimson. "Sorry, sir," Kincaid said.

"Fort Reno, in the Indian Nation. I'll wire Number Nine and let your captain know."

"I understood that these Cheyenne were to be settled here," Kincaid said, looking from Danner to Travers. "They have been promised that."

"We simply don't have the room, the materiel, or the manpower, Kincaid," Danner said peevishly.

"It was one of the prime reasons these Cheyenne offered to surrender, sir. To be here where their kinsmen were settled."

"It's hardly your place to criticize policy, Lieutenant."

"I agree, sir. But these people—they'll never take it, sir."

"They won't be told for a few days, Lieutenant Kincaid," the Indian agent put in. "Once they're used to the idea that they are embarking upon a new life, I don't think it will matter much to them whether it's here or in Oklahoma."

"Oh, but it will, sir. The old chief, Dull Knife, is for peace. He has promised his people a life here, in a land not so different from their own, among friends and relatives."

"We do not have the room," Danner said, and in his tone was an implicit order to butt out.

Kincaid could see it only too clearly now, and it scared him, just plain scared him. They had made a promise to the Northern Cheyenne that they never meant to keep. A promise to induce surrender. After the papers were signed, the Cheyenne would be told that, regrettably, they would have to march to the Indian Nation to be settled.

And when that time came, what would Little Wolf do? He would seem a prophet. He would crow about it, snatching influence from Dull Knife, railing against the treachery of the whites—and he'd be right.

"I wish we did have the room, Kincaid, but we don't," the agent said.

And they hadn't had any more room when they first agreed to settle the Northern Cheyenne here. Kincaid was angry, but there was absolutely nothing to do about it as they had told him so pointedly, it was hardly his decision.

The thing that unsettled him was the knowledge that Easy Company would be forced to help escort the Cheyenne southward. Tell *that* to the men. That fuse inside Little Wolf was getting damned short. Blood would come of this, and Kincaid knew it.

He waited until the wire was sent to Number Nine and an answer received, and then went out. A sour disgust was working in his belly, but he tried to ignore it. He managed pretty well until he had again crossed the parade. There, suddenly, he met Dull Knife and Little Wolf in full ceremonial dress.

Solemnly, Dull Knife said, "We go now to surrender. It is the best thing for all of our people. We see how content the Sioux are in peace." Then, incredibly and to Kincaid's complete embarrassment, the old chief stuck out a hand and said, "Thank you, Kincaid, for bringing us here. There was trouble, but that is past."

Kincaid took the dry, callused hand, glancing up to

see Little Wolf's contemptuous eyes on him. He looked away quickly.

Kincaid watched as the two Cheyenne chiefs strode through the crowded parade ground, heads held high. "There was trouble," Dull Knife had said, "but that is past." Kincaid only wished it were so.

He found his men and immediately informed them of everything. Their faces, flushed with relief an hour ago, grew stern, their eyes cold.

"See if I understand, sir," Malone said. "They're going to let the Cheyenne sign the surrender, believing they'll settle here. Then they turn the joke and tell 'em it's Oklahoma they're bound for. To top it all, we get to herd them south, while they get a good long chance to work themselves up in to a fury and rain fire and salt all over us."

"That's it in a nutshell."

"Jesus God! Wheeler was the smart one," Malone muttered.

"Go on now, have a few beers," Kincaid said. "Wash the dust out."

"I don't even have the taste for that now," Malone mumbled to no one in particular.

McBride was silent, but he shared Malone's feelings. It would take more than a few bottles of sutler's beer to wash the taste of this away.

"Sheep?" he said to Malone, but Malone couldn't even spare a smile for that.

"I think," Malone said after long consideration, "I'm going to get drunk, pick out a cavalry officer, and hit him in the mouth. See if they won't lock me up in a nice safe stockade."

"If it works," McBride said dryly, "there won't be enough officers to go around. Let's have some, Malone. Let's have some and sing a song and figure out what in God's name ever led us down this path of sorrow."

The others followed. Only Holzer, as blissfully ignorant as a child, was smiling. Matt Kincaid waited a decent interval, shaving and brushing his hair, before following his men across the dusk-shadowed parade. He would have a beer, maybe quite a few, himself, but it would be tasteless, unenjoyable. It was a dismal day, a dismal job, and the future held nothing pleasurable.

Yet, just as he thought that, he remembered something to look forward to with anticipation, and despite himself, Matt Kincaid began to whistle as he reached the plank-walk in front of Norm Braun's store.

seven _____

She was there, wearing a white apron over a pale green cotton dress. Katie Braun stood on a low stepladder, rapidly rearranging stock, from time to time checking a pad in the pocket of her apron.

Kincaid nodded to the knot of Easy Company men who sat or stood in the corner, hefting brown bottles of beer. Malone had his feet up on a barrel and already looked slightly belligerent. Someone, Dubois perhaps, had just finished the inevitable crack to Stretch about a tall drink, and it drew a respectable laugh.

A few cavalrymen stood near the doorway, glancing from time to time at Kincaid's "dragoons," as they termed his mounted infantry. It would be remarkable if the night passed without some sort of a ruckus.

Norm Braun was tending bar—which was what his counter seemed to be right now. The only trade in the sutler's store was in three-point-two, at this hour. Braun looked at Matt and then grinned warmly. He handed the six beers in his hands to the cavalrymen, wiped his palms on his apron, and offered his hand.

"Never thought I'd see you again, Lieutenant. What brings you here?"

Without elaborating, Matt told the sutler that they had escorted the Cheyenne to Robinson. Braun smiled slyly and leaned across his pine counter.

"So that's it. I thought maybe you'd been tracking

Katie." He winked and nodded to indicate his niece.

"Wouldn't be a whole lot of point in that," Matt replied. Braun leaned down, took out another beer, and opened it for Matt.

"I wouldn't say that. I thought she was kind of struck by you, Kincaid."

"Oh?" Matt took a drink. "I had a different view, I guess. Seemed a wonder she didn't strike me."

Braun laughed at Matt's weak joke and winked. "She's that way, you know. The men around here, why, they're put off too easy. She says 'boo,' and away they run. A man's got to be persistent, you know. She's a full-grown woman, and it'll take a full-grown man to topple her. 'Faint.heart...'" he quoted.

"She is a fair maiden," Matt agreed. He turned to watch a brief, playful flareup between Rafferty and McBride. "But damn it, man, if she's looking for a man, you'd never know it."

"No, and it's a damned waste." He fell silent. His wife walked past, exchanged pleasantries with Kincaid, and bustled on. "Woman like that. I'd hate to see a woman like my niece grow old and hard, develop one of them permanent ironclad hearts a man finds now and again. Somethin' happened to her after her folks was massacred. Maybe she had given them all her love and then it was snatched away. I don't know." He shrugged.

"Understand me, Kincaid," he added quickly. "I don't want to see her rush off and marry the first blockhead that comes through, and I sure as hell don't want to see her take up a dance-hall gal's life, but she's got love to give, and she's forgotten how to do it, how to give or receive. It's got her all blocked up, you know— Hell, I talk too much. There, she's done now, you could at least try a few words, huh?" He winked again and moved off down the counter to take care of a buffalo skinner who wanted a new knife.

Katie Braun stepped off her ladder, touched her hair, and half turned. She saw Matt, and her eyes opened wide and then narrowed sternly. Deliberately she placed the ladder aside and started toward the storeroom door.

"Good evening, Miss Braun."

"Good evening, Lieutenant—" she said, her voice dry as paper.

"Kincaid, still Kincaid."

"Yes." She turned away again, a mechanical smile on her full lips.

"I'd like to talk to you, Katie."

"My uncle is handling all sales just now," she answered, untying the apron behind her back.

"I didn't want to buy anything. Just thought we might talk."

"I can't imagine what we'd have in common." She folded the apron and tucked it under the counter. Behind Matt, a bottle hit the floor and broke.

"You never know until you try," he said to her. That got no reaction at all. "Have you eaten?"

"Not yet."

"Perhaps we could dine together."

"Maybe another time," she said. "Excuse me?" Again the quick, meaningless smile, and she was gone. She walked into the storeroom, her back straight, shoulders set, glossy dark ringlets bouncing, her hips moving from side to side no more than an inch.

Kincaid watched her until the door closed, and then he sighed, drinking his beer as he turned.

"Told you," the young officer he had spoken to said with a wink. "Cold as be-damned ice."

"Had to try for myself," Kincaid replied with a smile.

"Can't blame a man for that. Wish I knew how many times that door has been closed in my face," he said wistfully. "Take it easy now, Kincaid. I got a patrol going out."

Matt nodded goodbye and leaned against the counter, watching his men. He could have walked over to join them, but the conversation always tapered off, the laughs becoming less frequent.

A voice from the doorway rose in sarcastic comment just then. "Hey, fellas, looky there. Them boys got pretty little blue stripes on their pants. Kind of baby blue, don't it look cute?"

Kincaid glanced at the speaker—a half-drunk, big-shouldered corporal—and then he looked at Malone, who was grinning, gingerly placing his beer aside. Malone rubbed his hands together in anticipation and answered, "Hey, bigmouth, does that yellow strip stop at your asshole or does it run all the way up your back?"

Kincaid finished his beer and headed toward the door. An officer definitely was not wanted just now.

"You son of a bitch," the cavalry corporal called back, "I don't mind you insulting me, but don't say a word against the uniform."

"I got nothing against the uniform but the idiot that's wearing it," Malone cracked, still grinning.

"Well, by God!" the corporal said with mock regret, "I just don't think I can take no more."

Malone stood, rolling up his sleeves. "Sorry, yellow-leg, you're going to have to take it now. Come on over here, it you're as dumb as you look."

The corporal nodded and smiled himself, showing a gap where two front teeth used to be. Handing his own beer to one of his men, he shuffled over to Malone, eyeing him with derision. "You what a tough mounted *infant*-ry man looks like?"

"That's it, partner. Have a good long look, so you'll remember next time. It'll save you a whole lot of trouble."

Malone was loving it all. He positively had a taste for fighting, and one day it would probably get him killed. He liked the little game, the challenge and acceptance that went before it, savored wading in and giving his best licks. McBride took a deep breath and stepped aside.

The corporal was still smiling as he threw the first punch. Malone was pulling back, but it caught him above the ear, staggering him. He kicked the table aside and grinned. Behind the corporal, someone was tangling with Rafferty. Malone could catch none of the words.

"Come on, Corp," Malone said, spitting on his hands. "Let's see what you got besides a sneak punch."

The cavalryman waded in, and Malone was waiting for him. Malone tried a quick lead right, but it only glanced off the yellowleg's temple. The corporal retaliated with two hard left hooks. The first missed, but the second dropped over Malone's guard and caught him on the neck.

The corporal had left himself open momentarily, perhaps expecting a short, decisive fight. Recoiling from the hook, Malone had presence of mind enough to whip his own right into the corporal's ribs, and the big man grunted loudly as breath was forced out of him.

Malone bowed his neck and got to work. He came in with an explosive series of punches, going up and then down. He caught the corporal flush on the jaw with a right hand, then immediately dropped down to give him two hard body shots, and before the corporal could strike back, Malone had hooked him again to the head.

The corporal kicked out, trying to break Malone's kneecap, but Malone had seen this type of fighter before—rough, dirty, and unused to going any distance. He had been waiting for something like that. The kick gave Malone, time to slide his leg away, kick up with his own boot, and catch the corporal on the underside of his thigh.

The cavalryman roared with pain, clutched at his leg, and toppled over backwards. Malone followed him down.

Meanwhile, the second cavalryman was faring no better. The pack instinct had prompted him to try Rafferty. He had simply reached out and kicked Rafferty's chair from under him, and Rafferty had obliged.

Rafferty had done some boxing, something the yellowleg couldn't have known, and now he was slowly, methodically picking the man to pieces.

A straight left, then another, and a third, rocked back the yellowleg's head and Rafferty moved in, shuffling his feet, his knuckles held high. He feinted a left and the soldier jerked away almost in panic; his lips were already bloodied and pulped from the stiff, snapping jab Rafferty possessed. Rafferty followed his feint with a right, and the soldier, trying to duck away from the left that never came, ran right into it.

His eyes rolled back and he went to his knees and stayed there. Something crashed into Rafferty's legs and he fell. Malone and the corporal had rolled across the floor and into Rafferty. Now he was being drawn into the windmilling punches they threw.

Malone was bleeding from the nose. His shirt was nearly torn off, but he was still smiling. He hooked hard into the yellowleg's body, felt a rib crack, and hammered a left to the big man's face.

Rafferty, tumbling down, had kicked Malone in the face, and that straightened him up, turning on the lights in his head. The corporal leaped at the opportunity. Reaching up, he grabbed Malone by the ears and yanked, trying to crack Malone's skull against his own. Malone barely had time to shove his hand between their skulls.

It was painful and Malone thought he had broken his hand again, but it saved him from the disastrous result of a butt. Angered now, Malone shoved free of the corporal and rolled to his feet. Behind him the window smashed, and he ducked as he caught sight of a flying chair sailing past.

But he ducked into the corporal's fist, and his head snapped back violently. Malone shook if off and moved in again, hands held low.

McBride hadn't ducked quickly enough. The chair that had missed Malone slammed into the bugler's shoulder, and he dropped his beer.

"Goddammit, and here I was trying to be nice," Reb

98

thundered. He threw his hat aside and leaped across the table, taking two yellowlegs to the floor. From the corner of his eye he saw Stretch Dobbs draped all over a shorter, stockier opponent. The man was trying to shake him off, but Dobbs had him like a spider.

McBride was tossed aside by a huge cavalry private. His back slammed into the wall and he had barely regained his balance and wind when the big man came in on him. Big! He had a massive head that lolled on a bull neck, like a yoked ox. His shoulders were a foot through, from front to back, and he had forearms the size of McBride's calves.

Fortunately he was no fighter. He winged a wild right, which Reb ducked handily, and his fist punched an eight-inch hole in the sutler's plank wall. McBride brought a knee up hard into the yellowleg's groin and the man's eyes rolled back, his face went a pasty white, and he collapsed, groaning. Panting, McBride pulled away, only to be a met solidly on the back by a downward-arcing chair.

The chair caught him flush, and McBride went down hard, the wind driven from him, his mind on the fuzzy edge of consciousness. He managed to roll over to miss a stomping boot, but he knew he was a dead pigeon.

The boot came out of the darkness and landed on his head, and McBride grabbed at it, latching on to the soldier's trousers.

The leg was pulled away, and for a second McBride had a clear glimpse of the man's face. Dark, long, lantern-jawed. Just now it was malicious and quite drunk. The boot was lifted again and McBride could only lie there, waiting to take it as his head jumped with hot lights and his chest burned with pain.

Then, suddenly, the man was not there. A fist flashed out and tagged him squarely on the jaw. One swift, clean punch out of the Marquis of Queensbury's book, and the cavalry soldier went down.

McBride rolled his head and looked up to see a smiling

Wolfgang Holzer, as impeccable as ever, kissing his fist.

"Not to stomp on the people!" Holzer said loudly. His opponent never heard him. He was out cold beside McBride.

Holzer stretched out a hand and McBride took it. Then there were other hands, rough ones, lifting him to his feet.

The place was swarming with troopers now. Blinking away the haze, McBride could see a second louie, wearing an OD armband, standing hands on hips as they were herded out. Malone, finding himself beside his old adversary, threw a punch even as he was being dragged out in the arms of the soldiers.

McBride was rushed along toward the door. He saw the sutler watching with open mouthed dismay. Holzer, his hair in place, uniform straight, was allowed to remain where he stood.

But Wolfie objected. A stream of German poured from his incensed lips and he tapped himself on the chest. "I vas fight!" he insisted, and when they grabbed him as well, he grinned happily at McBride.

Katie Braun had the task of cleaning up the broken bottles, the splintered chair, the overturned tables, and she did it angrily, her movements quick and irritable.

"Soldiers," she muttered in disgust. Her uncle was nearby, examining the hole in his plank wall, and she looked up and said, "You see what I mean, don't you? Soldiers!"

"They're just big kids having a little fun," Norm Braun said. "Wish that big one hadn't hit the wall, though."

"Kids having a little fun," she echoed without looking up from her dustpan full of broken brown glass. "That's right! Big destructive children! Fun? Hitting each other in the face. A man could be seriously injured."

"Oh, not likely. They don't usually fight to hurt the other man. Besides, they all knew the officer of the day would break it up before it got too bad."

"How can you defend them, Uncle Norman?" Katie asked in exasperation, hands on hips, dish towel in her right fist.

"It's like this, Katie," he explained. "Those boys have been out on the plains where every day there's a chance of dying. The tension can get pretty bad. A drink and a fistfight—why, that's a way to let it off. I never yet seen a man draw a gun or try to use a knife. No, they don't want to hurt each other like that. All that business of cavalry hating mounted infantry, that's a bunch of nonsense too. It's just the excuse to start a fight. Each side knows the other does its share of fighting out there where it's deadly."

She shook her head. "I'll never understand men, and that is that."

"Maybe if you got to know some a little better," Norm suggested slyly.

"And don't start that again," she warned him. Busily she continued cleaning up before he could begin. Ever since that Kincaid had shown up here—why, a person would think she was a desperate old spinster or something, the way Uncle Norman went on. Kincaid! And what sort of an officer would just walk out and let his men go knuckle-and-skull with the local troopers? She didn't want to hear his name again. Not once more.

Katie glanced up suddenly. Her uncle was just standing there, leaning on a broom, a sparkle in his eyes, a faint smile on his lips, and for no reason at all she blushed. She felt her face growing hot, and it annoyed her. She turned her eyes away quickly, knowing he was still watching her, still smiling. Men! Damn them all!

Matt could have eaten at the colonel's table, as he could have slept in a bed in the BOQ, but somehow it seemed ignoble to do so. Danner doubtless thought of Kincaid as a hard-to-handle officer already, but Matt didn't really care. After breakfast in the camp, he sauntered to the

101

colonel's office and managed to get his men sprung, explaining that there was really no way they could assist in escorting the Cheyenne southward if the bulk of his detachment was in the stockade. Reluctantly the colonel agreed.

"Have you a time schedule on the move yet, sir?" Matt asked.

"The surrender will be signed sometime today—attend if you like—then, say, three days to rest their horses. Friday, it looks like. Dawn Friday."

"You haven't yet informed the Cheyenne chiefs?" Matt asked, and Danner gave him a heavy, unhappy look.

"Not yet, Lieutenant," he said, and his tone indicated that he was finished discussing the subject. As Matt turned to go, Danner called after him, "Keep those troops of yours under control, Kincaid. Another incident like last night and I will have to keep them locked up, consequences be damned."

"Yes, sir," Matt said. He was happy that Danner couldn't see the slow smile spreading across his face as he turned to stride through the orderly room and out into the bright, cool sunshine.

He stepped into the saddle and turned his bay toward the main gate, moving slowly through the crowd of Indians, traders, and soldiers.

He had nearly made the gate when he heard someone calling, and he turned in the saddle to see Norm Braun waving his hands over his head as he ran toward Kincaid, Matt held up.

"Lieutenant Kincaid..." Braun panted, leaning against the shoulder of Matt's horse.

"Something wrong?" he asked with concern.

"No. Not serious... I just wondered... you busy?"

"Doing nothing at all for three days," Matt told him.

"That's what I thought." Norm Braun took another minute to get his breath back. Then he began again, "I got no right to ask—I mean, you're army and on duty and all..."

"What is it, Mr. Braun?" Matt asked.

"I got a delivery needs to be made way out to Giles Fork. A family homesteading there. Thing is, Katie's the one I'd have to send—I'm busy as hell myself—and it's a long damned way for a woman alone. So I was thinkin' maybe a man who hadn't a thing else to do—that is, if it wasn't imposing..."

"It'd be a pleasure," Matt said with a smile. "I'd favor a ride in the country over sitting here."

"Good!" Braun rubbed his hands together. "Listen, then, the wagon is being loaded out the back door. An hour?"

"An hour's fine, Mr. Braun."

Braun retreated, still beaming, and Matt smiled, wondering how he was going to handle the second half of his plan. Returning to camp, Matt shaved and found a fresh shirt, which he buttoned as Wojensky watched him speculatively.

"Take charge of things, will you, Corporal?"

"Yes, sir. Begging the lieutenant's pardon, but could a man ask where the lieutenant is going?"

"He could indeed. I'm going courting, Corporal. Going courting."

Matt smiled and tossed his towel to Wojensky, who could only stand and stare after him as he walked back toward Fort Robinson.

"He can't pick it up," Noram Braun said for the fourth time. "His wife's sick, so take the wagon on out there, Katie. This is no time for arguing. Do you work for me or not?"

"I work for you," Katie said with a sigh as they walked through the store room. "But darned if I can figure you out, Uncle Norman. Every time I've suggested taking a load of goods out to one of our customers, you've

103

insisted it was too dangerous out there. Now, *boom!*"

"A man can change his mind, can't he?" Braun said glibly.

The back door was open and light streamed in, glaring blue-white. It blinded Katie until she was nearly to the wagon. She checked the tarpaulin and clambered into the box, tying her bonnet.

Before she could react, the man in the army uniform was up beside her, reaching for the reins. She squawked a complaint and grabbed for the reins herself, but Matt snapped them and the wagon lurched into motion, nearly toppling Katie from the spring seat.

She struggled to regain her balance and sat up, flustered and mad as a wet hen.

"Kincaid!"

"Hello." He grinned, and her flush deepened. Turning, she could see her uncle standing, arms akimbo, grinning his fool head off.

"A trap! A dirty male trap. A kidnapping, with my guardian's approval. Damn it, stop or I'll jump!"

"I can't stop," Matt said soberly. "And I wouldn't jump. We're going fast enough that you might break a leg. That wouldn't be worth it."

"It might, to get away from you."

"You've obviously never broken a leg." Matt slapped the reins again, and the horses, already moving briskly, flattened back their ears and raced across the dry grass plains toward the cottonwood-lined river beyond.

"This is disgusting!" Katie screamed. "And you can slow down now. I'm not going to jump, and it's too damned far to walk back."

"Cuss a lot for a lady, don't you?"

"That's none of your damned business either," she shot back, her black eyes sparking. Matt smiled, infuriating her, and she sat, arms crossed beneath her breasts, until he hit a bump and she had to scramble to hold on.

He gradually slowed the team, and turning to her, he said, "Look, Katie, I know your uncle set this up. But

104

he only wanted us to get out and have a little conversation, maybe learn something about each other. He meant no harm. I can turn around and take you back if you want—I don't usually kidnap young ladies. On the other hand, there's a load of groceries back there that a family needs. It's got to be delivered, and I haven't a halfwit's notion of where Giles Fork is. I'd likely spend half the day looking and have to come back without having delivered the load. Very bad for business, wouldn't you say?"

"What do you suggest?"

"Only a truce. You don't have to talk, don't have to look at me. We'll deliver the goods and I'll drive you back, and that'll be the end of it."

"It is business," she said dubiously.

"Sure."

"Wouldn't make sense to go back." She turned toward him. "But you won't try any foolishness?"

"Like what?"

"Don't play stupid—man stuff."

"Not if you say not. I am an officer and a gentleman."

"You've got the shoulder straps to prove you're an officer, but I'm not so sure about the other, Matt Kincaid."

"No!" He laughed. "Well then, that's something we can discover on this trip, isn't it?"

She half smiled, cocked her head, and then looked away, having nothing else to say on the subject.

The day was pleasant, and it was cool near the river, where the wind worked in the cottonwoods, turning their leaves silver. Matt kept to the side of the rutted road when possible, keeping the dust down. The matched grays moved silkily, and although Katie wasn't much of a hand with the social graces, he enjoyed being beside her, watching the sun on her dark, shiny hair where it escaped her bonnet, the soft scent of her, part sun warmth, part woman-scent, part jasmine—faint and intriguing.

At noon they reached Giles Fork and the squat, sod-roofed house that stood there. A woman in an apron and a gingham dress, her face prematurely lined and harsh, her hair knotted back severely, came out to greet them.

"Pleased to see you're feeling well, Mrs. Pyle. Heard you were feeling poorly," Katie said. The woman just shook her head, pondering it.

"No," she said finally, "I ain't been sick. You got my flatiron in this load, Katie? Surely been waiting for it."

"Sorry, not in this one," Katie answered. "Had to be ordered from St. Louis."

As she talked, Katie Braun deftly untied the tarpaulin and began carrying the goods to the porch. She was graceful, even carrying those loads, and obviously stronger than she looked.

Matt hopped down to help, and Mrs. Pyle looked at him worriedly. "Ain't no Indians kickin' up, are there?"

"No, Mrs. Pyle," Katie answered. "Lieutenant Kincaid is just a friend of my Uncle Norm who's thinking about quitting the army and getting honest work."

"Oh?" Mrs. Pyle scratched her head. "Do tell," she muttered.

On the way back, Matt said, "You really didn't have to make that crack about the army, did you, Katie?"

"True, isn't it?"

"Not at all. The army has its faults—glaring ones, sometimes. And people jump on those faults, maybe because the army's looked upon as public property, as a hole where tax dollars are thrown. But there are many thousands of people out here who would be dead if it weren't for the army."

"And thousands of others who would be alive."

"That is the truth, a sad truth. But nations are colliding on the plains, and when nations collide, there is killing. You should know that better than anyone," he reminded her.

"The army didn't help my parents."

"No, but it has helped others like them. I don't really understand what you have against the army," Matt said, "unless it's the fact that there are so many men in it."

She turned and opened her mouth to speak, but did not. Matt was slowing the team, and now he turned them toward the river.

"What are you doing?" she demanded.

"Team's thirsty. I thought I'd let them have a drink. What's the matter, Katie, don't you like horses, either? You should favor these. They're both geldings."

"I knew you were no gentleman!"

"No. Well..." Matt said, pulling the team up as they reached the river, "sometimes it takes the presence of a lady to bring out the gentleman."

"Yet another insult."

"I suppose." Matt helped her down. "But you show a tough hide to us, Katie. No man likes to be slapped down. Turned away, all right, that's your privilege, but not slapped down like a dog mounting your leg."

"God, you're coarse too."

"That, as a woman once told me when I pointed out that she cussed a lot for a lady, is none of your business. I'm just an errand boy for the sutler. Doing my job. You can't expect much of me."

The horses drank, lifting their muzzles now and then. The sunlight, streaming through the cottonwoods, silvered the droplets on their muzzles as they lifted their heads. A crow, cawing angrily, sailed across the cloudless sky.

She was next to him, unspeaking, rigid, and he turned. He had no intention of doing it, had every intention of avoiding it, in fact, but something made him take her in his arms before she could turn away, and press his lips to hers.

Her fists were upraised, clenched tightly between them, and her scent was in his nostrils. He kissed that voluptuous mouth, finding it as unyielding as her personality. He held her, his mouth touching hers lightly at each corner, before he kissed her fully again.

Suddenly her lips softened and melted to meet his, and then, just as abruptly, they went hard again and she pushed him away with her fists, her face still with anger.

"Damn you! And you ask why I slap you away like a dog. You are like that little dog—all of you!" She touched her lips as if he had bruised them, and turned suddenly away, looking at the river.

Matt went back to the wagon, climbed into the box, and lifted the reins. He waited for a long minute. She turned again and walked slowly to the wagon, hoisting her skirt to step up.

Slowly, Matt urged the horses into motion and turned them homeward. The ride was silent, deadly silent, and Matt regretted having kissed her. She stared straight ahead, nearly motionless, until he pulled the wagon up behind her uncle's store.

Then she practically vaulted from the wagon and rushed inside, past a smiling Norm Braun. A greeting died on Braun's lips.

"You!" she said to him. Then, sputtering, she hoisted her skirts and rushed past him.

Braun watched her go and then turned, scratching his bald head. "Get the delivery made, Kincaid?"

"Made the delivery," Matt assured him. Then, more quietly, he added, "But I don't think you ought to call on me for help next time."

"No? That bad, huh?"

"That bad," Matt answered.

"Sorry about that, Lieutenant. I thought maybe . . ." He shrugged.

"Yes. So did I," Matt replied. "It's not your fault, though, Mr. Braun," he said, shaking hands. "It was probably mine. Probably all mine."

Braun scratched his head again and stood watching as Kincaid strode back toward Easy Company's camp.

Smoke rose from the Cheyenne tipis, and Matt deliberately avoided looking that way. He didn't want to think about it today.

Wojensky was sitting near Kincaid's tent, doing some saddle repair work, and the corporal glanced up from his needle long enough to ask, "How'd the courting go, sir?"

"Not well, Corporal. Not well. The lady said that as far as she was concerned, it was only puppy love."

eight ═══════════════

Major Halstead had drawn command, and he approached through the low ground fog, riding his milk-white gelding. "Morning, Kincaid," he said.

"Morning, sir. Ready to move them?"

"Just about. Your men will ride drag."

"All right." Kincaid smiled to himself. It was kind of the cavalry to let Easy Company eat the dust. "How are they taking it?" he asked, meaning the Cheyenne.

"How do you think?" Halstead asked. He looked around and then said in a lowered voice, "Nobody asked me what I think of this, either, but I'll tell you, Kincaid— it stinks. It's a hell of a way to treat them, betraying our promise. Who in hell is going to believe an army assurance next time?" He started to turn away and then added, "If you ever mention that I said anything of this sort, we'll have to go at it with sabers, Kincaid, because I'll call you a liar."

Since Easy Company was to bring up the rear, Matt sat his horse, watching as Halstead led them out. The Cheyenne filed forward, faces blank, eyes unfathomable. They had been told they were home. Now, after three days, the army had decided differently. They would be marched south to the Indian Nation, where the land was dry and the incessant winds blew dust, where there were no elk and no far green mountains, where the rivers ran muddy and the summer baked a man's brains, where

111

they knew no one, and no one cared if they lived or died.

Dull Knife rode past slowly; he had given his word that the Cheyenne would at least look at the Nation for Indians. But he felt deeply betrayed, that was obvious from his expression. And Kincaid, whose hand he had taken in gratitude so recently, was one of those embroiled in treachery. He wore blue, he was the enemy.

It had always been that way, and now it looked as though it would remain that way for a long while with these Cheyenne. The last of the Indians moved silently past, the dust pluming into the air to settle over the Robinson agency slowly, marking their passing. Dust soon settled and unremembered.

Kincaid lifted a hand and heard McBride and Wojensky shout out the commands behind him. They were the last sounds he heard for a time. Slowly they rode in the wake of the Cheyenne, looking down the long, long trail, knowing deep in their hearts that now there was no way out, that the blood they had feared all along would flow, and flow freely.

She stood at the warehouse door, a shawl around her shoulders, and watched the soldiers until she could see no more. Then she turned to find her Uncle Norman standing behind her, and she hoped to God he wouldn't make a joke.

He didn't. He put his arm around Katie's shoulder and walked her back into the shadowed store, closing the door behind them.

Southward they rode, and the days grew longer and dustier. The sun was hot on their backs, the dust always in their nostrils, their ears, their mouths. Uniforms were plastered to their bodies; their throats were sandpaper, their eyes layered with grit. And they were silent. Every man waiting, waiting for the moment when the guns would have to be unlimbered and the death toll taken.

They camped on the North Platte, not far from Horse Creek. Brittle, weary men, they slumped to the ground

112

and drank their coffee sullenly in the near darkness. The sundown was mirrored in the waters of the Platte—orange and deep, deep violet. No one seemed to notice it, as no one heard the larks singing, the ceaseless grumping of bullfrogs in the reeds.

Stretch Dobbs spoke from out of the darkness, and it seemed he spoke for all of them. "Boys," he said, "I don't think it'd bother me at all to go along home," and they knew that by "home" he meant Outpost Number Nine, where the air was much cleaner.

At sundown they found them. Gus Olsen instantly raised his hand and pumped his arm twice. The two renegade Indians were camped below them, along the coulee. They were drinking from a stagnant pond.

This was the second day of the hunt; the young bucks had slipped away from the agency, killed three of Tom Butler's cows, and set fire to his barn. Panicked, Butler had reported the "uprising."

Windy Mandalian inched up beside Olsen and nodded. He did not speak or even whisper—sound carried too far. Instead the old scout, in moccasins, slipped ahead, moving in a crouch, circling to the south to block off any escape.

Herman Javitts and Private Robinson moved to the far side of the coulee, while Gus and Corporal Miller held their position.

Robinson, who had only been in the army three months, stuck close to Javitts, trusting to his leadership. After all, Javitts had experience and a reputation. The captain had written him a letter of commendation for bravery, for his actions during the night attack by Hal Blodgett and his gang of renegades.

That raid, and Javitts's part in it, were regular bunkhouse fodder. They said he was a shoo-in for corporal on the next list, with Conway standing behind him.

Javitts lifted a hand and Robinson went to his belly. The Indians had slipped away from the water hole and were now dog-trotting up a small feeder wash. Javitts beckoned Robinson forward and the private had a clear view of the renegades. He was surprised at their youth. They couldn't have been more than sixteen or seventeen.

Javitts let them draw nearer, watching them weave through the willows and leap the rocks along the bottom. The clicking of Javitts's pistol was clearly audible.

The young renegades were directly below now, and Javitts came to his feet, his pistol leveled. As Robinson watched, the renegades' eyes opened wide and they halted, fatigued and frightened. They threw their lances aside and raised their hands high.

As Robinson watched, Javitts slowly squeezed the trigger of his Schofield, and one of the renegades was slammed back, his chest blown open. The second Indian tried to run, but Javitts fired twice more. The first bullet hit him high in the shoulder, turning him, and Javitts's second shot ripped into his abdomen, splashing the sand with blood.

"Took care of those bastards," Javitts said, reloading.

"They were surrendering!" Robinson said, choking.

"You believe that? It was a trick, Robinson. You've got to shoot first, boy. If you don't—look at my face again."

Robinson did, seeing the mass of scar tissue, the tattooing of black powder. Still...by God, they were trying to surrender. Javitts slid into the wash, Robinson behind him. Coolly, Herman Javitts retrieved their lances and placed them in their dead hands.

He turned one of them over, and Robinson saw the gaping, leaking hole in the Cheyenne's guts. He turned around and was sick. Herman Javitts watched the kid puke and he smiled. Miller was coming at a gallop, Windy and Sergeant Olsen behind him. Herman Javitts stood, legs spread wide, a smile on his face, watching them.

"Get 'em?" Miller asked, swinging down. His face

was sweat-streaked, smeared with dust. He saw the two renegades immediately.

"I got 'em," Javitts replied.

"Had to kill 'em?" Miller asked uncertainly.

"They were tryin' to jump the kid," Javitts lied. Robinson turned around, started to open his mouth, and shut it again, looking goggle-eyed at Miller.

"What happened?" Gus Olsen asked, swinging down from his horse. Javitts repeated the lie and Olsen nodded, examining the bodies. The first man had been shot once, the second front and back. Probably Javitts had gotten him in the stomach and he had whirled away, taking the second shot in the back.

Gus straightened up, grinning. "By God, Herman, you did it again. You're getting to be a hell of a soldier, boy." Gus slapped Herman on the shoulder and, turning to Robinson, said, "I guess you owe this man your life, but you're not alone in that."

Robinson stood there on rubbery legs, his expression one of anguish. Olsen smiled; the kid was badly shaken. Well, Javitts had once been like that, and now look at him. "Let's pick 'em up and tote 'em in," Olsen said. Then he looked at the renegades again, recognizing their youth. "Damn shame they had to fight—nothin' but kids."

That was what Windy thought. It surprised him that they had fought. It wasn't usual. Young bucks jumping the agency, they most often rode free for a time, raised a little hell, pulled a few shenanigans to impress the young ladies, and when surrounded they usually surrendered, knowing the worst in store for them was a little time in the stockade.

But these had fought. Why? Lances against sixguns. Windy felt a sour suspicion growing in his throat. Looking at Robinson, he wondered again. The kid had started to say something. What? Javitts was strutting in his best cock-of-the-walk manner, and Windy, turning his head, spat a stream of tobacco juice. Miller seemed not to have noticed anything unusual. Gus had, but he must have believed he was wrong; after all, Herman Javitts was a hero. The captain had said so, standing him up in front of all the company.

He'd saved Flora and Maggie, saved Ben Cohen's hide, saved Miller and Wheeler and Rothausen, as well as all the stores in Pop Evans's place. The man was a hero. *Maybe,* Windy thought with growing conviction, *he likes that feeling a mite too much.*

"I don't understand what you're driving at," Captain Conway said when Windy reported the incident. "Javitts said the renegades were trying to jump the kid. Did you see different?"

"No sir." Windy leaned back in the chair, drinking the captain's whiskey. Flora was pretending to sew, but her attention was on the conversation. "It was a feeling, sir. Somethin' was wrong there."

"If I spoke to Robinson, you know what I'd get."

"Yes, sir, I do." Mandalian put his empty glass aside and recrossed his long legs. "You'd get the same story Javitts tells. A man don't report his pals. Thing is, I thought you should know anyway. It may come up again."

After Windy had gone, Conway turned soberly to his wife. She met his eyes and shook her head worriedly.

"Windy's probably mistaken, dear," she offered.

"I don't think so. He doesn't poke his nose into army business unless he's damned sure. I believe him." Conway was silent. Leaning against the wall, he crossed his arms. "The thing is, what do we do about it? We took a solider who, if not cowardly, was definitely under-aggressive, and we made a hero out of him. He responded under pressure and—well, you know what he did. Everyone congratulated him. I wrote him a letter of commendation. I'm trying to wangle a medal for the man!

116

Now just how in God's name, after having made him into what he is, do we slap him down?

"And who's to blame, Flora? Tell me that—who exactly is to blame?"

It was a dry month, crossing Kansas. The winds roiled the dust constantly. Water was seldom available. But the Cheyenne, under close guard day and night, made no move to break away. Weaponless, they had no choice but to ride on across the dry, flat land.

Finally, blessedly, they reached the North Canadian and followed it; they were in the Nation. From time to time they ran across mounted patrols of Indian police, mostly Cherokee, and here and there they saw houses of all sorts: some build of brush and sod, a scattering of tipis, a few really good log houses—though where the lumber had come from, Kincaid couldn't guess. The Oklahoma plains were treeless and arid, dry and barren. The Cheyenne looked like people being escorted through the gates of hell. Their faces were anguished or frightened, some simply uneasy, others outright mad. Like Little Wolf's.

Kincaid reckoned they had a right to be all of that, and more.

At least they had the small consolation of knowing that Easy Company would be going back to Number Nine by morning. They had not asked him about the fairness of this; if he suggested something, he would be ignored. He could do nothing to help, and so the most he could do was ride away and try not to think about it—but he had an idea the memory would be a long time dying.

Fort Robinson was a bit of heaven, compared to Fort Reno. It sat squat and tilted against the dry plains, buffeted by wind, washed by dust. Even the Canadian River, flowing slowly past, seemed murky, dusty, dry.

Dull Knife had advised his people to at least view the

117

Indian Nation—it was that or war, a war they could not possibly win. Now they had seen it. Possibly the land was acceptable to the southern tribes, to the Comanche or Kiowa who had roamed such territory from time immemorial, but to the Cheyenne, used to crystal streams, long grass, and mountains, it was a crushing disappointment.

Maybe in time, Kincaid thought, *they can adjust to it, be the farmers the government wants, settle in and learn. Maybe.*

The Cheyenne, to everyone's relief, were immediately taken over by troops from Reno, and by Indian police who moved in to stand guard. These haughty, stone-faced men in blue uniforms were entirely capable of handling the Cheyenne, as well as every other bit of disturbance across the Nation.

The Indian agent, a man named Clark, who dressed in white linen and wore a cork hat like the one General Crook favored, moved immediately among the Cheyenne, interviewing them, counting heads, the young Indian in American dress behind him writing down the vital information.

"Cut the boys loose, sir?" Wojensky asked. His dust-coated face was broken by a smile of relief.

"Wait until I can report in," Kincaid decided. "Tell them to get shaved and washed, though. I expect they've got beer here somewhere."

"Yes, sir," Wojensky answered with a snappy salute, turning his horse away, his smile growing broader.

"Going in?" Major Halstead asked, walking to where Kincaid was loosening his cinch.

"Guess we'd better. Who's the CO?"

"Landers. A light colonel. Know him?"

"No," Kincaid answered.

Halstead nodded absently. Kincaid doubted he had heard his reply. The cavalry major was standing, looking out across the field where the Cheyenne were gathered, and Kincaid knew his thoughts. He also knew that Halstead would say nothing. He had blurted out his feelings once, and that was once too often for a hard-nosed career soldier.

"Let's go on up," Halstead said. "I'm ready to get back to Nebraska."

They found Lieutenant Colonel Landers in his office. A narrow, birdlike man with snapping eyes and a thin white mustache, he welcomed them warmly, offered drinks, and perched on his desk as he talked to them, taking their report.

"Thank you very much, gentlemen," Landers said when they were through. "It's been a long hard trail, I imagine. Why don't you avail yourselves of our officers' club. It's quite a good one, really, might surprise you."

"Thank you, sir," Halstead responded, "but I'm under orders to return as soon as possible. I take that to mean now."

"All right, sorry about that, Major. But Lieutenant Kincaid, you'll have time while you are awaiting orders."

Kincaid's head jerked up. "My orders were to proceed to Fort Reno, sir. No further instructions."

"Assigned to Major Halstead, were you?"

"Unofficially, sir, I suppose."

Landers sighed, smiled amiably, and spread his hands. "I really can't release you, Kincaid. You know the army; I'll need orders cut. Halstead?"

"I know nothing more than Kincaid does, sir," Halstead said with a glance of commiseration. "I had assumed that Colonel Danner would wire orders, or that Captain Conway at Number Nine would have gone through Regiment."

"Unfortunately no, not yet."

"May I wire Captain Conway, sir?" Kincaid asked.

"Of course, of course," Landers said with another smile. He was a likable man, Kincaid decided, but every bit as army as Halstead was. No orders, nothing moves.

"I'm sure this can be straightened out in a few days," Matt said.

"Oh, I'm sure it can," Landers agreed as the three officers rose. "Although I hate to see you go. I assumed, perhaps wrongly, that your detachment was being loaned to me through the summer. We've had a bit of trouble on the eastern line and, by God, we're shorthanded." He hastened to add, "But I won't try to keep you to your post's detriment."

They said their goodbyes and Halstead walked out onto the parade with Matt. "Sorry about the foulup, Kincaid," he said. "Glad it's not me. Thanks." He offered his hand—red, tough as leather, thick and strong—and Kincaid took it.

Kincaid watched him go, and then, shaking his head, turned toward the telegraph office, which, at Reno, abutted the paddock for some inexplicable reason.

Opening the door, he found three harried men—two of them Indians—scribbling furiously, sorting stacks of papers, thrusting them into saddlebags.

"Sir?" the white man said, looking up.

"Need to send a telegram," Matt said.

"Doesn't everyone?" the man sighed. "That's what these are," he said, indicating the papers before him. "Except the renegades cut the telegraph wires ten miles out, and everything has to go by horse pouch."

"For how long?"

"No tellin', Lieutenant. Last time, they burned twenty miles of posts and sniped at the crew that went out to replace 'em. A week? A month?" he shrugged.

"By God!" Kincaid clenched his fists and leaned across his desk. Then he sighed, recovering himself. "Don't you think the CO ought to be informed of this?" he demanded.

"Colonel Landers?" the man's face was a mask of puzzlement. "Why, he knows, sir. He's known for two days."

Kincaid laughed despite himself, and shook his head. What was it the man had said? *I assumed your detachment was being loaned to me for the summer.* . . . It looked as though it was. Matt stuck out his hand and asked, "Can you let me have a pencil and a form? I want to send a horse-pouch message to Outpost Number Nine."

"Outpost Number Nine? Where is that sir?" the clerk asked, handing over the yellow form.

"Wyoming," Matt said.

"Wyoming? I'll be damned." The clerk scratched his head with the stub of a pencil. "Be an almighty long time getting there, won't it?"

"All summer, it looks like," Matt said, shaking his head again. "Very likely all summer."

The boys were brushed and polished when he got back to camp. Wojensky met him, saying, "I told them to take it easy, sir. They will—no one wants to be left in the guardhouse when we ride out, and not many of them are foolish enough to want to make the ride with a big head."

"Good." Kincaid only nodded. He looked over his detachment. "Cut 'em loose," he told Wojensky. Tomorrow he would tell them. Tomorrow would be soon enough.

nine _____

The summer dragged by. Dry, endless days with the air heavy with dust, broken only by the angry, boiling tornadoes that swept through twice, one touching down within five hundred yards of Reno.

Easy Company's duties had not changed appreciably. They were still standing guard over the new arrivals. Among the newcomers, breakout attempts were common, and they required extra watching.

"Think they'll make it?" McBride asked Malone, who had been sitting his horse in the meager shade of a dead cottonwood tree, watching the Cheyenne scratch at the earth, trying to plant a cornfield in that parched clay. Now Malone stretched his arms mightily and looked at McBride.

"Hell, I don't know, Reb. I keep thinkin' how I'd like it if someone told me I had to become a dirt farmer, like it or not."

"Some of 'em seem to do fine. Saw a Sioux over yonder with a nice batch of cattle."

"Some of 'em do fine," Malone agreed. That was the end of the conversation. It was too dry for jawing. McBride uncorked his canteen, took a drink of the tepid water, nodded, and moved on.

Malone stretched again, rolled up his sleeves, and turned his own bay southward. He followed the dry riverbed for a mile, listening to the constant hum of insects, waving his hand before his face to chase the gnats. When he could stand no more of that, he lit the half cigar he had stowed away in his shirt pocket and rode on, puffing out clouds of tobacco smoke to discourage the bugs.

He pulled up abruptly.

He had only a glimpse, and then the man was gone. Just a flash of buckskin among the cattails. It had to be an Indian, and whoever he was, he was well over the boundary. Malone unslung his rifle with a smooth, practiced sweep of his arm and, holding it overhead, kneed his bay forward into the bog, where the cattails grew to eight and ten feet.

He rode a zigzag pattern among the cattails, his horse sinking to its knees as it worked through the mat of brush.

Nothing. He began to doubt his own vision. Sitting utterly still, he stubbed out the telltale cigar and tucked what was left away. The faint breeze rattled the cattails. A loon fluttered away.

And then he heard it—someone splashing across a stretch of water. Malone heeled the bay to his right. The Indian was still moving away from the agency, still trying to lose himself in the bog.

His horse moved ahead, stepping lightly. And then Malone dug his spurs in. There he was.

Malone leaped his bay through a screen of brush and pursued him. Breaking clear, he got a better view and smiled to himself.

It was a squaw. A young one too, and not bad looking. Her face turned back to measure Malone as she ran, carrying a bundle beneath her arm. What she saw was that he was nearly on top of her, and she must have realized she had no chance, but she ran on anyway.

Malone had managed to hang his rifle back on its spider even as he rode, and now, as he closed on the woman, he was able to simply lean out, hook her under the arms, and yank her off her feet.

Simply! He had her swung off her feet, but she writhed like a wildcat, shrieking her head off. Suddenly she clamped her teeth into the base of Malone's thumb, and his own yowl answered hers.

"Hold it! Hold on! I'm not gonna hurt you." Her teeth were still locked on to his hand, and Malone drew up his horse and reached down with his free hand, trying to get her to release.

He clutched at her chin and throat, but it was useless.

"Jesus!" Malone yelled. Lifting her bodily by the chin, he swing his leg across the horse's withers and dropped to the ground with her, rolling down the small slope to the bog, where they promptly sank in eight inches of muddy water.

She hadn't faltered in her dedication to biting his thumb off, so Malone used his last resort. He took her by the hair and held her head under water for what seemed an incredible length of time.

"Let go, dammit! Let go!"

She hung on so tenaciously that he thought she would drown before she let go, but finally he felt her teeth part and she came up gasping and choking, her hair across her face, smeared with mud.

"Jesus, can you bite!" Malone breathed. He looked at his hand, saw she had gotten him nearly to the bone, and winced.

In that moment she scrambled to her hands and knees, panting as she watched him and then took off. Malone shot to his feet and went for her in a long, low dive.

He hit the Indian girl at the calves and dragged her down, her face going into the mucky bog again. She writhed like an eel, and he fought to hold her, taking care to pay special attention to those teeth.

"If you'd just hold it a damn minute—!"

"You go hell yourself, soldier man!" she spat, and then twisting free, she tried to run again. She hadn't left Malone much choice in how to handle this.

He reached out, grabbed the back of her dress, and spun her around. At the same time he cocked his fist and planted a letter-perfect left hook on the point of her jaw. She went down like a wet sack.

"Sorry, woman," Malone muttered. Reaching down, he grabbed hold of her muddy, profuse hair and turned,

125

dragging her up out of the bog, his uniform sodden.

He lay her down beside his uncertain horse and snatched his canteen off the saddle, rinsing the mud and slime from his mouth. Then he removed his shirt, shaking it until the worst of the mud was off it.

The woman hadn't moved an eyelash. Malone took a long look at her. Her dress had ridden up, and what he could see of her calves were shapely, golden, lithe. She had wide, sure hips and a small waist; her breasts, full and firm, revealed themselves plainly beneath the buckskin.

Her nose was a little wide, her mouth a trifle small. But all in all he saw a hell of a good-looking Cheyenne woman, and he felt a momentary tremor in his loins.

Shaking that off as being beyond the call of duty, he hung his canteen on the pommel and squatted on his heels, waiting for her to come around.

After a few minutes an eye did flicker open and her lips parted, revealing good teeth, a pink tongue. She moaned, rolled her head, and opened her eyes, looking dreamily at him for all of five seconds before she sat bolt upright, fury exploding in her eyes.

"You bad soldier man!" she shouted. Then, holding her head, she sagged back. Malone was smiling at the terrible dressing-down she had given him; but then, he figured, "bad soldier man" was probably the worst thing a Cheyenne could call you.

Her eyes were open, but she seemed to have calmed some, resigned herself to being captured. She shaded her eyes with her forearm and told him, "Head hurts."

"Sorry—the only way I could stop you. Want a drink?"

She nodded and he got the canteen. He squatted on his heels, watching her drink. When she was through, he rinsed his thumb off, sucked at the still-flowing blood, and showed it to her.

"Hand hurts."

A faint smile trembled on her lips. "Why did you stop me?" she asked, looking away.

126

"It's my job, woman. Why did you want to run away?"

"Why!" She started to sit up abruptly, then controlled herself and came slowly up, eyes hard once more. "Because there is no food, because there is nothing but misery here. I want to find a hunter, a man, a Cheyenne man who will marry me and take me away."

"You'd have to look a mighty far piece for a wild Cheyenne," Malone said. Then he recollected what she had told him, and he asked her, "What do you mean, there's no food?"

"I mean there is nothing to eat on the agency. No food," she said, as if Malone were dim.

"There has to be food," he said with a shake of his head.

"There has to be food, yes! Yes, there has to be food if we are to live, but there is no food! They give us none. Little Wolf says—" She shut up suddenly.

"What does Little Wolf say?"

"Nothing. I don't know." Now she tried to rise, but she was still woozy. Malone told her to stay down.

"There's always supposed to be food, woman. What is your name, anyway?"

"Dawn Cloud," she said, as if giving away a secret.

"All right, Dawn Cloud, now I ain't nothin' but a private soldier, but I know there's got to be supplies coming in for you people. If you're not getting them, talk to the agent."

"We have talked to the agent."

"Then talk to the army."

"We have talked to the army," Dawn Cloud said, wiping her tangled hair from her face. Her fingers, Malone noticed, were long and tapered, callused from work, but altogether attractive.

"Listen, are you hungry now?" he asked, rising.

"Always we are hungry."

"I've got some grub in my saddlebags," he offered, moving toward them.

"No!" She was angry again. Puzzled, Malone looked at her.

"Why not?"

"I eat no food of yours. I know you—I saw you before. You brought us south."

"I was there," he admitted.

"I will not eat your food. I am sorry I drank your water. What do you take me for? Lay-down-for-white-man?" she inquired. Malone took it that meant some kind of a whore.

"I don't take you for nothin'. I was just offering. You don't want it," he said, growing angry, "don't eat it."

"Then I will not."

"Good!"

"I am not like my sister, you know."

"How the hell would I know? I don't know your sister."

"Mountain Star's wife. The one who slept with the white soldier."

"The hell you say! Is that what happened? I figured so."

"Did he not tell everyone?" she asked, astonished.

"No. He never did. But your sister told all the Cheyenne?"

"Only me," she answered. "A deep shame. She was married to a good warrior, too. Brave man!" she said, thumping her own ample chest as if she were every bit as brave.

"Maybe brave," Malone retorted, "but not too damn smart, was he? Can't say he was much of a fighter, either, come to think of it."

"He was smart! Like a fox," she argued, and Malone answered:

"He was smart, he wouldn't of stolen that horse, wouldn't of jumped Rafferty, wouldn't of got himself killed." After a pause, Malone added, "If he'd been all that smart, he would've married you and not your sister."

"What do you mean!" Now fully alert, ready for trouble again, she stood with her hands on her hips, tapping her toe.

"I mean you're a damn fine-lookin' woman, Dawn

Cloud. He didn't see that, he wasn't too smart."

She could find no reply to that, and so Malone went on, "Now we got business to do. You got to go back to the agency. You can come along on your feet, or I'm afraid I'll have to pop you on the chin again and carry you across my saddle. 'S up to you."

"What do I care? Hit me again!"

"You know I don't want to. I don't want to have to drag you back, either, but it's my job, and I'll do it. But I'll make you a promise. This business about the food. I'll tell my...chief about it. He's a good man, Dawn Cloud, and he'll see that whatever's gone wrong is set right."

"How can I believe that?" she demanded.

Malone winked and answered, "You can believe it. I'm tellin' you it's so."

"Why would you do this?" she wanted to know, softening a little bit.

"Because it's right." He stepped into the saddle. "Maybe because I helped bring you down here, and I feel a little responsible."

"Maybe I almost believe you, soldier man."

"Call me Malone. Pick up your pack now, and I'll help you up behind me." She did so reluctantly. "No, not that hand," Malone said with a grin. "Here." He stretched out his left and drew her up behind him, where she rode silently as the bay crossed the creekbed and walked across the plains.

"Here," she said at last. "Let me down here, so they do not know I ride with a soldier."

Malone drew up and she slid from the horse's back. He touched his hatbrim and turned to go. He was nearly out of sight before he heard Dawn Cloud call after him, "Malone! Maybe you are not such a bad soldier man!"

Malone pulled up and turned to see her hightailing it across the plains toward the agency. He smiled softly; damned if that wasn't one of the finest compliments he could remember.

It reinforced his determination to ask Lieutenant Kincaid to look into the Cheyenne complaints. But he knew what Kincaid's reply would be.

"It's really not in our area of responsibility, Malone," Matt told him. He stood and walked around his room in the Fort Reno BOQ.

"I know that, sir."

"This informant of yours"—Malone had somehow never gotten around to mentioning that it was a woman—"he is sure that something is wrong?"

"My informant thinks everything is just the way the army has planned it, sir. That's Little Wolf's line to them, and they believe it. Just because some thief is stealing—"

"Easy, Malone," Kincaid reminded him, nodding in the direction of a seemingly sleeping cavalry officer in a nearby bunk.

"Thing is, sir, if there's truth to it, we owe it to them to find out, don't you think?"

Kincaid nodded. He did think so; the only problem was, what right did he have to poke his nose in? But if the supplies were being delayed or diverted, it was criminal. The Cheyenne wouldn't take much more. Already there was an epidemic of the ague, brought on by the new climate. Many young children had died, many old people. The ague, the post surgeon had explained, was a malarial disease, and the afflicted Cheyenne showed all the signs of malaria: fever, chills, severe abdominal pains. The surgeon had also informed Kincaid that it hit the northern tribes especially hard, and that the army and the Indian bureau damn well knew it.

"I'll look into it," Kincaid promised. "Probably get my hands slapped, but then that's a small enough price." He changed the subject. "The Cheyenne you spoke to said that Wheeler definitely had an Indian woman?"

"That's what the Cheyenne said, sir. Seems Mountain Star found them together and jumped Wheeler."

"Then why didn't Wheeler go to the captain and tell

130

him? Damn, it beats being on the desertion list."

"I reckon," Malone agreed. "But you recall how things were, sir. Captain Conway had laid the law down. Maybe Wheeler figured Conway would turn him over to the Cheyenne, or else he figured the girl would talk and they'd cut his throat."

"If I know Captain Conway," Kincaid said in exasperation, "most likely Wheeler would have been escorted back to Number Nine and punished later. Now—damn it, if they find Wheeler, he's liable to be shot."

"A man gets scared and he runs," Malone said with a shrug. He stood and picked up his hat. A young cavalry lieutenant had come into the BOQ, and Malone could tell he was not wanted; things weren't like they were at Number Nine. An enlisted man did not cross that threshold.

Kincaid escorted him out onto the plankwalk. The sun was low in the skies, painting long shadows. "It might be a good idea, Malone, if you were to maintain contact with your informant, if that's possible."

"It could be, sir," Malone said without expression.

"It wouldn't hurt to have eyes and ears in the Cheyenne camp. Since Windy pulled out, we have no way of knowing what their thinking is."

"I'll do my best, sir," Malone said, saluting.

"I know you will." What was that faint smile on Malone's lips? "And I'll do my damnedest to discover the situation on these supplies. Make sure your informant believes that, Malone."

"I will, sir."

Then, with a nod, Malone was gone, and Matt Kincaid was left on the plankwalk. He frowned heavily, turning matters over in his mind. He wasn't going to come out of this looking good. A temporarily assigned first lieutenant wouldn't make himself too popular by bullying the Indian agent, practically accusing the army of mismanagement. But there was no other way—no decent way.

131

Might as well get to it, he told himself. Returning, he retrieved his gunbelt from his bunk, catching a lazy eyelid lifting to observe him. Then he was gone, out into the cool evening, watching the cookfires being kindled across the plains.

Kincaid saddled his horse and walked it across the parade to the sutler's store. Entering, he nodded to some of the officers he knew casually, moved to the end of the counter, and waited while the sutler's helper took care of a sergeant who was buying one of the many Indian blankets there.

He heard enough conversation to discover that the blanket was bound for a sister in Ohio. The sergeant had hopes that it would reach there by Christmas—three months away.

Finished at last with that sale, the sutler moved to where Kincaid waited.

"Help you, sir?"

"Ten pounds of sugar," Kincaid said.

The sutler's assistant lifted an eyebrow but said nothing—"Sell 'em what they want," old man Butler was in the habit of saying. What the lieutenant wanted with sugar was beyond his comprehension, but he dragged ten pounds from the shelf and slapped it onto the counter.

"That looks light to me," Kincaid said, and the sutler's helper sighed mightily.

"All weighed. It's ten pounds or over."

"What do you weigh it on?" Kincaid asked. The clerk nodded toward the big iron-and-brass scale with the scoop bin in the corner.

"Mind if I see for myself?"

"Whatever pleases you," the clerk said with obvious irritation. Maybe the CO had had some complaints, and this officer was checking them out. Well, he'd find nothing. Butler never shorted a man. At the prices he charged, it was hardly necessary. "Give 'em a little extra," the old man was fond of saying. "Makes 'em think they're getting a bargain."

Kincaid slapped the sugar bag down on the scale, adjusted the sliding weight, and nodded. Ten pounds, two ounces. "Satisfied?" the clerk asked dryly.

"Very. Thanks for your help." He paid for the sugar and added a quarter for the clerk. "For your trouble."

"Well." The clerk's graciousness returned with a rush. "Thanks Lieutenant."

Kincaid shouldered the bag, waved a hand, and walked past the vaguely curious eyes of the Reno soldiers. Outside, he tied the sugar onto his horse and stepped into leather. It was ten miles to the agency, and it would be full dark before he got there. Good, Kincaid decided.

The night was pleasantly warm, but mosquitoes were everywhere. He startled a feeding coyote on the plains and the animal ran off, yapping excitedly, leaving its dinner, a jackrabbit, on the ground. Kincaid smiled. The coyote would simply run in a circle and return to its feeding, only its digestion disturbed.

There was a pale crescent moon rising, looking like a fingernail paring, and a single low star hung in the west, blue, brittle, hypnotic.

It was two hours to the agency, and Kincaid steered toward the beef pens, now empty, and the adjoining office. A candle or lantern burned low in the rickety building, and that disturbed him.

Swinging down, he walked onto the swaying plank-walk, holding the sugar bag in one hand. The man inside was young, no more than twenty, at least half Indian— Cherokee, Kincaid guessed.

"General inspection," Kincaid said without announcing himself.

"Mr. Turnbull ain't here." The Cherokee was shaken.

"No matter. You can show me around. Frankly, these inspections are always a waste of time. I'll be gone in fifteen minutes."

That seemed to relieve the kid, and he had started to offer a tour of the place where the beef was purchased,

133

accounted for, and consigned to the Indians. Kincaid was abrupt.

"Scales first, please."

"The, uh . . ." The kid swallowed hard. "Without Mr. Turnbull . . ."

"Listen, do I have to bring the inspector general himself by?" Kincaid bluffed. *What* inspector general he couldn't have said, but the kid was appropriately impressed. He unhooked a key from a wall bracket and said, "This way, sir."

Kincaid followed him into the feeble moonlight of the pens, his eyes searching the shadows. *Kincaid, you can be as much a fool as any of your men at times,* he told himself.

The low barn smelled of dung and slaughter, with a strong overtone of lye disinfectant. "All clean and neat," the Cherokee said.

"Yes. Open up, please."

Inside, the Indian tried to show Kincaid the stalls, the meat hooks, the butcher's implements, but Matt wasn't to be deterred; he walked directly to the huge scales, under the Cherokee's dolorous scrutiny.

Matt reached up and hung the sack of sugar on the meat hook. He adjusted the weights and smiled thinly. Innocently he turned to the Cherokee. "I can't seem to operate this scale properly. According to my reading, I have five pounds of sugar here. I happen to know it's ten."

The Cherokee fumbled nervously with the sliding weights and explained, "Sometimes the lighter weights . . . this scale is meant, you see, for whole beeves."

"Oh?" Matt nodded belief. Suddenly his face brightened, "Then, just to clear matters up, you hang on it."

"Sir?" the Indian swallowed hard.

"Sure, just so we can get on with the inspection. Here," Matt removed the punctured sack from the hook. "You hang on that."

"But I—" Matt's face tightened and the man moved

134

dutifully forward. He was a narrowly built man, as tall as Matt's six feet, but not so broad in the shoulders. The scale read eighty pounds. "Jesus," Matt exclaimed. "You must be missing a few meals, son."

"It's—" There was no explanation. The kid unhooked himself and wiped his hands on a nearby rag.

"Let's see your books now," Matt said coolly.

"I can't, sir. Only Mr. Turnbull can do that. He's the contractor, you see."

"But he's not here, son. I am. I would like very much to leave your name out of my report if possible, Mr. . . ."

He swallowed again. "John Littletree."

"Mr. Littetree, I would like very much to leave your name out of my report. If it became common knowldge that an Indian was engaged in defrauding his own people, actually letting them go hungry"—Matt shook his head— "well, it could be quite serious, couldn't it?"

"This way," Littletree said quickly.

The books were wide open, revealing plainly the finagling that was going on here. Six hundred three-year-old Texas steers: net butchered weight a hundred and fifty-six thousand pounds. Two hundred and sixty pounds of beef per head. He hoped those Texans had been paid by the head.

Kincaid glanced up at Littletree, and the kid had to turn his dark eyes away from him. It looked as though Turnbull had stolen two-thirds of the cattle intended for Indian consumption. No doubt the contractor was a man of considerable means by now; what did it matter if a few Cheyenne were slowly starving to death?

And if it went this way with the beef, what else was going on at this agency? Kincaid deftly tore the page from the book, to Littletree's astonishment.

He walked out and mounted again, turning his horse northward, lifting it to a gallop. By God, he thought, I can't do anything about Indian policy, but I can damn sure break this open. But how, he wondered, had they avoided finding out before this? That gave him pause.

135

He slowed his horse, feeling his spirits deflate. He might be walking into a hornets' nest here, but by God it had to be done. And if there was some sort of conspiracy, all the more reason to do it. The ride back to Reno seemed much shorter, much colder.

To Malone, conversely, the night seemed exceptionally warm. It could have been her warm thighs surrounding him, or the soft globes of her breasts against his chest, or perhaps the excited, urgent breathing in his ear, the way he was compelled to keep his body moving, thrusting into her hot slipperiness, rocking her back and forth. It could have been any of those, but there was no doubt it was a warm night.

It hadn't started out that way. She had been cool when they first met, pleased that Kincaid was going to try to look into the food situation, but not overly optimistic.

Then, for no reason whatsoever, her eyes had misted over, shimmering in the moonlight. Malone had put his arms around her and it had begun, accelerating, snarling, like a downhill spill into wild confusion, arms and legs everywhere, sweet pungent scents, earthy and animal. The rapid caress of a callused hand against soft flesh, the throbbing, the long kisses, the probing tongues, the compelling suckling of taut nipples thrust into his face as hands groped for his hot, throbbing erection.

"Now, now..." Dawn Cloud murmured, and pulled away from Malone. "Now this way. Please me. Bury yourself." She got to her hands and knees, her hair hanging to the ground, and Malone mounted her from behind, spreading her with this thumbs as he eased forward. She guided him in inch by inch, her head hanging low so that she could look between his legs, see his shaft sliding into her, see the taut sack between his hard-muscled thighs. Her hand met his, and they grappled, touching her moist inner flesh, his rock-hard erection as he drove it home.

She rolled her head from side to side, lifting herself higher to give him access, inviting him to split her, to climb inside, to fill her and cause her own juices to burst forth, flooding him.

Malone was intent on his work. His hands rested on her white, moonlit buttocks, feeling the rippling of muscle there, the tiny satisfied quivers.

Her hand was at his crotch again, clutching his scrotum, holding him deep inside while she writhed on him like an impaled, wild thing. Then he felt her give way, felt her come undone, felt the oozing moisture, the clutching of tiny muscles inside her honeyed sheath, and he could hold back no more.

Her hand still held him, stroking him as he leaned far forward, grabbing at her breasts, mauling them roughly, as he mashed his pelvis against her ass, riding her savagely, driving her face against the ground as he reached for a climax that was coming now, coming with a slow ache, a pulsing, hard need.

"Now, Malone. Now, you bad soldier, fill me. Please. Please." Her voice was close to tears, but her quivering body fought his in a rage of need. She pawed at him, her breath coming in hot, desperate gasps, until he felt her begin to quiver, to release tiny, panting sounds like those of a captured bird.

She went flat against the earth suddenly, and Malone was climbing over her, wanting to crawl inside her. On his knees behind her, he threw back his head in concentration and slammed against her, feeling the last climactic tremors before he fell exhausted against her, still quivering, kissing her back, her shoulders, her sleek neck beneath the veil of dark, rich hair.

He lay there a long while, feeling the residual tremors of her body as it cooled itself and regained a more natural rhythm, her heart slowing to a dull pounding, her blood racing less madly to the demanding parts of her body.

She rolled away when he least expected it, and stretched out her arms to him. He kissed her and traced patterns around her breasts. She smiled, and the moonlight gleamed on her teeth.

"Very nice for such a bad man," Dawn Cloud said softly.

"Try again for luck?" Malone asked.

"I think you have not seen a woman for a long time, Malone."

"I think you are right, but I'm almost glad I had to wait for you."

"Then you liked it?" she asked almost shyly.

"Damn right." He kissed her again.

"Malone—" She was looking away, her hand on his strong arm. "How far are we from the agency?"

"Far enough that you don't have to worry about being caught," he said.

"Yes, but how far?" She gripped both of his arms and searched his eyes.

"Maybe ten miles." He kissed her lips and nuzzled her ear. "What say we try again?"

She laughed out loud. "Such a man you are!" As he persisted, kissing her mouth with more ardor, she said, "All right, all right, yes, my soldier, but first I must get up for a minute, go to the river."

"Sure." Malone lifted an eyebrow and rolled aside, reclining on the blanket.

He watched her rise, liking the way the moon gleamed on her lithe body. She turned to go, hesitated, and came back, leaning low to kiss his forehead, her hand lingering on his shoulder.

"Right back," she said, and he noticed her eyes filming over again.

"Sure." Malone lay back, hands behind his head, listening to the river sounds. Then there was a sudden explosive sound that did not belong. A horse running toward the river. He sat upright with a lurch. "My goddamned horse!" he shouted, realizing what he was hearing.

Malone leaped to his feet, grabbing at his gunbelt. Some dirty son of a bitch had his horse. "Dawn Cloud! Dawn Cloud!"

He heard his horse splashing across the river—and it *was* his horse, he could see it plainly now. He could also clearly see the rider. It was Dawn Cloud, and he lowered his pistol.

"Where are you going? Dawn Cloud! For God's sake, bring that horse back!"

But she didn't stop until she had reached the far side of the river and merged with the shadows.

"I didn't want you to get hurt, Malone!" she called out cryptically. Then she was gone. Malone heard the slowly retreating hoofs and he stood there, numbed.

"Well, goddammit all!" He turned and nearly threw his pistol down before training and common sense made him keep his grip. He snatched up his pants. "Don't want me to get hurt?" He shook his head. "What in hell does that mean?" The woman was crazy, plain crazy.

He dressed and sat on the blanket, waiting. Maybe it was some kind of a prank, and she would return, laughing. But he sat there for an hour as the night grew chill, and Dawn Cloud did not return.

"Damn her," he muttered. "I guess I paid for that tumble."

He snatched up his rifle and the blanket, figuring the night might grow colder. And she had had the nerve to ask how far the agency was, so she damned well knew. Ten miles.

"You didn't want to hurt me," Malone said again, repeating her words with wonder. "There's damn sure going to be one part of me hurtin'—my fuckin' feet, after I walk ten miles."

Sourly he started forward, wading across the river with his boots tied around his neck. Then, emerging from the trees that lined the river, he stood looking across the dark plains. With a heavy, heavy sigh, he started forward.

"Not only do I fail to see what this page from Turnbull's ledger proves, Lieutenant, but I have grave reservations about the manner in which you obtained it. Presenting yourself as a government inspector, bullying the Indian—"

"It was underhanded and likely not strictly legal," Kincaid admitted, "but the man is cheating the Indians. There are people out there who are sick and hungry. I frankly didn't give a damn about the legalities, sir. I was concerned about the Cheyenne."

"Yes, I quite understand, Kincaid," Landers said, wiping his hand back across his thinning white hair. "But utilizing such deceptions—"

The colonel was interrupted by a harried-looking captain who rushed into the officers' club, eyes searching the small, felt-topped tables until they settled on Landers. He rushed to the table, holding the saber at his side.

"Sir, beg your pardon. Most urgent!"

He whispered into Landers's ear, and Kincaid saw the expression on the lieutenant colonel's face pass from intense interest to fury.

"Damn it all to bloody hell!" Landers said, coming so abruptly to his feet that he nearly toppled the table. "It appears it's too late for all of your concerns, Kincaid," he said. He held the crumpled ledger sheet balled up in his hand. Loudly he announced to the roomful of officers, "Boots and saddles, gentlemen. The Cheyenne have jumped the agency!"

ten

Before Kincaid could even reach his quarters, he had the story from Wojensky, who had heard it through the grapevine an hour before the colonel got his message. The Cheyenne had parlayed and agreed that this land was no good—there was no food, and the evil spirits of the place were making them all ill. Dull Knife had apparently bowed to Little Wolf's demands that they leave, and they had done so, sometime after midnight.

A short detachment of fifteen men had tangled with the Cheyenne up near Kingsford Wash and been soundly defeated. The Indians were well armed and had deadly intentions. Little Wolf had sent a message via one of the wounded soldiers, saying they would fight to the last man, and if the army intended to make war, they had better let the Cheyenne first get out of the Nation, or the ground there would be so saturated with blood that no corn would ever grow there again.

"What caused the delay?" Kincaid wanted to know. He was saddling rapidly.

"The breakout was reported to the OD, and he figured to handle it without disturbing the commanding officer. It was the OD's idea that fifteen men could handle the breakout. He hadn't been informed fully, and underestimated the size of the Cheyenne party."

Kincaid nodded his understanding. Someday, he told himself, he was going to figure out a way to keep as well informed as the enlisted men.

"All of our men present and accounted for, Corporal?"

"All except Malone. He had an overnight pass."

"The devil he did. And where would a man go on an overnight pass around here?"

Wojensky only shrugged.

Easy Company had come on the run, McBride still pulling on a shirt, his gunbelt slung around his neck. Landers hadn't reappeared after rushing into his headquarters nearly fifteen minutes earlier, and Kincaid's horse sidestepped impatiently.

Two cavalry companies had formed up raggedly, and now and then a confused shout was raised. Nothing moved. The men waited, shifting and milling.

Another half hour passed before an officer appeared on the plankwalk and motioned to Kincaid, who stepped down and entered the headquarters himself.

Landers and two of his men were standing studying the map, drinks in their hands. Kincaid was astonished, but he composed himself.

"They've got fifty miles on us," Landers was saying. "Oh, welcome, Kincaid. We've just been reviewing the situation. Seems madness to go rushing after them in the dark, wouldn't you say?"

"Not necessarily, sir, there's a lot of ground to be made up—"

Landers interrupted him with a laugh. "I told you Kincaid was a firebrand, Frank."

The curly-haired, young-looking captain smiled around his cigar. "We've decided to wire Fort Supply," the captain said. "Have them seal off the area north of the Canadian. "We'll start out fresh and fully supplied tomorrow."

"Squeeze them right between our forces," Landers said.

"Yes, sir," Kincaid said. Just how in hell the troopers out of Fort Supply were going to "seal off the area" was beyond Kincaid. There were nearly three hundred Cheyenne on the march, but they knew the art of concealment well. The problem was, Landers wasn't treating this as a problem in tactics at all. Oh, well, at least Kincaid had learned that the telegraph wires were up again, however temporarily.

"I want your men rested and ready for pursuit in the morning, Kincaid."

"Yes, sir." Easy Company again! God, were they doomed to live forever with these Cheyenne?

"I don't foresee any trouble in returning them to the agency," Landers said. Only he said it a little too casually, and Kincaid thought he saw the reason why they were being allowed to draw away from the area. There would be fighting, and Landers knew it. But such a fight must not be viewed by the other settled tribes. They must not see soldiers killed by Indian guns. On the other hand, Landers didn't want the "tame" Indians to see the Cheyenne chopped down by army guns; that could only result in cold resentment.

Whatever his motives, orders were orders. Kincaid bade them a stiff good night and returned to his men.

McBride had just finished dressing, and Kincaid had to smile faintly. "Dismount them, Corporal Wojensky. We're starting out in the morning."

"Sir?" Wojensky cocked his head curiously. "Did I hear you correctly?"

"Sleep in the barracks tonight. Full packs in the morning. This is liable to be a long chase, Corporal. Make sure," he added, "that every man has extra ammunition. We may find we'll need it."

"Yes, sir." Wojensky saluted sharply, dismissed his men, and unsaddled his own horse, watching Kincaid, who stood alone, deep in thought. He knew what the lieutenant was thinking—it was in all of their thoughts.

They had brought the Cheyenne here, to this place of sickness and hunger. They had deceived the Indians. Now they would be following them, and when there was fighting, it would be their fingers that squeezed the triggers and brought them down.

It was hard duty, and Wojensky decided it was better not to think about it.

Malone stamped into the barracks an hour before dawn, and Wojensky, who had not been able to sleep well, crawled from his bunk.

"What's the matter?" the corporal asked. Malone had yanked his boots off and now just sat there miserably, his gear at his feet.

"Nothin'," he growled.

Malone started to lie back, and Wojensky warned him, "Better not even fall asleep. We're riding in an hour."

"Not funny, Wojensky," Malone answered. Then, studying the corporal's face, he saw that the man was serious. "Where?"

"The Cheyenne broke out of the agency. We're going to get to tag along after them."

Malone whistled. "No shit?"

A thoughtful expression came over his face, and suddenly he nodded.

"What is it?"

"Nothin'. An Indian stole my horse, Wo. I didn't want to say anything, but that's what happened. I just walked in ten miles." She'd stolen his horse because she figured there would be fighting; that was what she'd meant—*I don't want you to get hurt.*

"You all right, Malone?"

"Sure. When they took off—there was no fighting?"

"No." Wojensky shook his head. "They got clean away. But I'll tell you, Malone, there'll sure as hell be fighting when we catch up with them. They won't come back here voluntarily."

"No, they sure as hell won't." Malone frowned. "Damn, Wojensky, we know quite a few of them people now. Christ, we've been with them—"

"Most of eight months," Wojensky supplied. The two men's eyes met with understanding, and then they looked

144

away, not wanting to drag the discussion on, to probe the sensitive areas.

Malone massaged his feet for a while, put on dry socks, and then, with a sigh, stamped into his boots again, forcing the hot, swollen feet down. Then he sat there, closing his eyes, feeling his body nagging at him, demanding sleep. He stood abruptly. "I'm going to see how much coffee I can drink, Corporal."

Wojensky nodded authorization, and Malone staggered toward the door. Outside, he stood for a minute, smelling the early morning, watching the last of the stars before he walked toward the mess hall.

He saw, or thought he saw—in the shadowed light it was difficult to be sure—Lieutenant Kincaid standing on the plankwalk in front of the BOQ. Malone dismissed the notion. If it was Kincaid, what was he doing up? And he had been simply standing there, staring, not even noticing Malone as he walked near.

They rode out with the dawn. The sun was an orange ball hanging behind the screen of low, thin clouds to the east. There was no sound but the chinking of saddle fittings, the squeak of leather, the occasional muffled cough. The horses cut a wide green band across the dew-silvered grass. Captain Frank Ketchum was in charge of the company of cavalry and the squad of Indian police; Kincaid's detachment was the remainder of the force, which numbered two hundred and twelve fighting men.

The day grew hot and the trail clearer. The Cherokee scouts could follow the Cheyenne tracks nearly at a run, but Ketchum held them to an easy walk. He was in no hurry, and some of the men, aware of the situation, wondered if he didn't want the force from Fort Supply to do the fighting—if fighting there was to be.

Kincaid rode somberly, his face wooden. They were heading northward once again, but it was nothing like he had hoped the return trip would be.

145

At noon they found the burned farm.

The grass had been fired, and the house as well. From the porch, a woman who had been dragging out a few scorched belongings waved her hands.

"You're a little late, aren't you?" she demanded angrily.

"Indians?" Captain Ketchum asked.

"Of course it was Indians. My husband's away on a cattle drive. Just lucky I saw them coming. My girl and I"—she nodded to the blonde moppet who hid behind her mother's leg—"hid in the haystack. It's a wonder they didn't set fire to it too."

"What did they take?" Ketchum asked. He was all business.

"Horses. My man's guns, all the food they could carry. Who were they? They had women with them. Kids. What kind of raiding party it that? Why can't the army protect us?"

She unleashed her flurry of questions for another five minutes, venting her anger. When they rode out she was still standing, hands on hips, watching them.

Ten miles farther on, they found the second farm. These people had not been so lucky. Ketchum had six men dig the graves for the man and his wife and four children.

When they rode on, there was a slow anger building in Ketchum, and he was not alone. The pace lifted, almost of its own volition. No command had been given, but they rode on more quickly, through the dusty heat of the day, across the long Oklahoma plains.

At sundown they met the troopers from Fort Supply.

"Damn!" Ketchum said, loudly enough to be heard all the way back to the tail of the column. He knew now that all Landers's plan had accomplished was to give the Cheyenne time to outrun the pursuit.

The captain in charge of the Fort Supply contingent was no older than Ketchum, but Kincaid recognized the hard, plains-wise cut of the man. The man was angry, and not concealing it well.

"They got through, then," Ketchum said.

"Looks like it." The captain mopped his head. "You every try to patrol a thousand-mile line with forty men?"

"You saw nothing?" Ketchum persisted.

"Nothing. Mind telling me just how in hell you managed to lose three hundred Indians in the first place?"

There was no answer to that, and Ketchum sputtered and looked away. "They can't be far."

"No," the captain from Fort Supply agreed. "But it's the finding of them that's tough, isn't it? We'll accompany you as far as the North Canadian. Then my orders compel me to return to my post."

Without even a salute, the captain turned back toward his men, leaving Ketchum fuming. He called one of his Indian scouts to his side and scribbled a message.

"I'll notify every post between here and Wyoming. By God, those savages won't get far."

He folded the message and handed it to the Cherokee, who took off at a dead run, his long black hair flying. Then he looked at Kincaid.

"What else can I do?" he asked.

"Nothing," Matt answered. "Nothing at all."

They made dry camp on the plains and were moving again at dawn. They lost the Fort Supply contingent that day, but finally picked up the Cheyenne trail. The Cherokee scout believed they were at least twelve hours ahead.

Yet they could gain no ground, and on the third day following, with the horses and men exhausted, they had to break off pursuit and veer toward Fort Wallace, near Sand Creek, Kansas.

Fresh horses were not available and had to be requisitioned from a rancher thirty miles to the north. The wagon was refitted, and fresh and well supplied, they rode out of Wallace.

"Only three, four days behind," Stretch Dobbs grumbled. "And no sign of their trail."

"Don't matter," Malone said, nodding toward the long trail before them. "We know where they're headed. They're going home, Stretch. Going home where the long grass grows."

Dobbs fell silent, nodding, and Malone settled into leather. He still felt sympathy for the Cheyenne, but that sympathy was fading as the long trail became a trail of bloodshed and depredation. Little Wolf was giving his anger free rein. Six times they passed ranches that day; all six had been attacked, three of them burned.

The Cherokee scouts had been riding wide, and in the early afternoon the man called Tom Bear reported in.

Kincaid rode over to hear his report.

"They are slowing now. Horses weary. Two parties, I think," Tom Bear said, habitually motioning with his hands.

"Two parties? Little Wolf's and Dull Knife's?" Kincaid wondered.

"I think so," the Cherokee said with a shrug. "Maybe one day hard ride, maybe two." He shrugged again.

"All right." Ketchum's face was set now. He was weary and he was angry. Angry at the long ride, at the killing he had seen, at being taken for a fool. "We'll make it a hard ride. Let's close that gap."

"Sir?"

Captain Warner Conway looked up from his desk to see Sergeant Cohen standing there, a telegram in his hand. "What is it, Ben?"

"An alert from Regiment, sir." Ben shook his head. "I'm not sure I can explain it, you'd better read it for yourself."

He did, and the puzzlement on Cohen's face spread to his own. The Northern Cheyenne they had escorted southward had somehow jumped the agency—men, women, and children—and were now riding north. His own Easy Company detachment was in pursuit, and Conway was ordered to put a force in the field.

"Sweep the area between here and the Niobrara. If contact is negative, report to Colonel Danner at Robinson," he read aloud, then looked up at Cohen, who had regained his stony self-control.

"How in the hell . . . why, in God's name?" Conway glanced again at the telegram, as if rereading it might produce fresh insight. It didn't. "Have Sergeant Olsen and Corporal Miller report to me, Ben. Roust Fitzgerald and let me know when Taylor gets back off patrol."

"Yes, sir. Will the captain be taking command of the detachment?"

"Yes, Ben, I will. I was in at the start, I want to see the finish. I don't understand a bit of this. I didn't understand it when the Cheyenne were trailed to the Nation. Now they've jumped the agency. Why? I'm going, Ben. I want to know."

"There's also a civilian here to see you, sir."

"Important?"

"Could be. He's got a small place down on the Beale Wash. Grows corn, or tries to. He's had someone hanging around, stealing food, a coat, things like that."

"Agency Indians?" Conway asked.

"No, sir. A white man. He saw him once, plain as day." Cohen paused. "And from the description, sir— it sounds a hell of a lot like Private Wheeler."

"The hell you say!"

"Want to talk to him?"

"You bet I do. Send the man in, Sergeant."

Conway talked to the man, a narrow, tobacco-chewing sodbuster. He had, he said, tried handling it himself, but he didn't have the time to chase vagrants all over the territory. Of one point the man was certain: the thief was wearing army blue—torn, faded, but still identifiable as an army uniform. The description matched Wheeler's.

There was no figuring that one out either, and Conway didn't try. There was too much else going on. Fitzgerald arrived within minutes, Miller and Olsen not far behind him.

"Mr. Taylor will stay to command the post," Conway told them. "We will leave him sufficient personnel to assist him." He didn't need to mention the Blodgett raid specifically; they all knew what he was referring to.

"We will try to make our departure at dawn, gentlemen. I'll have Rothausen prepare an early breakfast. Let's use all the light we can."

"Sir?" Gus Olsen interrupted tentatively. "I was wondering if you could give me some sort of an explanation about what happened. It's a puzzle to me."

"No, I can't give you an explanation," Conway replied. "I don't understand it myself. All I know is that we took a party of nearly three hundred friendlies and turned them into a pack of bloody hostiles."

eleven _____

They found them at dawn, straggling across the Platte toward the mountainous sand dunes beyond. Kincaid looked that way, toward the mile upon mile of dunes where an army could lose itself, where horseback pursuit was absurd. Then he looked back toward Frank Ketchum.

The Cheyenne were still more than a mile off; there was nothing for it but to charge, and try to cut them off before they made the dunes.

McBride was still carrying his bugle, and Ketchum beckoned to him. Kincaid's heart was thumping as he placed a hand on his pistol. It was here suddenly, the time they had all dreaded, the battle they had ridden eight hundred miles to fight.

The enemy was down there, and among them were friends. But there was no way of knowing which was which. McBride's bugle cut through Kincaid's thoughts. Clear, sharp, the familiar sound was a demanding call to battle, the death song.

Kincaid could see the Indians, still in two distinct groups, momentarily freeze and then ride frantically toward the dunes.

At the charge, Ketchum fired the first shot as they drove down the bluffs, spilling onto the flats like blue-clad death. Kincaid chased his bleak thoughts away. This was battle and he was a soldier. There was no time for regret.

Little Wolf's own cavalry turned, fired a staccato barrage, and wheeled away, Easy Company in pursuit. Kincaid saw a Cheyenne go down hard and be trampled by Indian ponies.

Beside Kincaid, a man jerked and clutched at his chest; there was no mistaking who it was. Stretch Dobbs had been hit, his lanky frame perhaps too large a target.

Kincaid searched for Little Wolf and found him. The Cheyenne warlord was wearing paint, and he had daubed his red pony with the stuff.

Little Wolf's face was outlined in blue, smeared with black around the eyes. Like some death's-head demon, he motioned frantically to his people, directing the flow of the battle.

Kincaid aimed a shot his way and missed wide. His bay leaped a downed cavalry soldier, completely spoiling his aim, and when he looked again the angle was wrong.

A shot whiffed by within inches of Kincaid's ear, and he fired back at the nearest brave. The man crumpled and disappeared beneath the pall of black powder smoke that was settling over the battlefield.

Malone saw Stretch Dobbs hit, checked to make sure he was alive, and then fought on with a vengeance. He emptied his first pistol as quickly as he could fire it. The targets were close, stationary, and firing back nearly into his face.

Under the cavalry onslaught and the flanking attack of Easy Company, however, the Cheyenne fell back rapidly, and Malone took his time with his second pistol and definitely put down two Cheyenne braves.

The first was a head shot, and the brave was dead before he hit the ground. The second was through a warrior's leg and into his pony's shoulder. The pony crumpled and rolled, throwing the badly injured rider.

Malone reloaded on the run, losing his hat to the wind or a too-near bullet. A third of the Cheyenne force had wheeled to hold off the charge of the bluecoats, while the others made for the sand dunes. A hail of lead and arrows descended on the pursuers. Malone felt his horse stagger and go down, and he kicked free of the stirrups, landing hard on his shoulder.

Holzer sat in the middle of the whirling maelstrom and, using his rifle methodically, picked off three Cheyenne. From the corner of his eye he noticed that Ketchum's second squad had encircled Dull Knife's band and they had surrendered to a man, but Little Wolf fought on. Dobbs went down, then a nameless cavalry soldier, then Malone's horse was shot from under him.

Holzer turned and saw a Cheyenne on foot, blood streaming from his face, rushing at Malone with a raised hatchet. Holzer fired and the Indian buckled. Malone looked up from his reloading in time to see the Indian fall nearly at his feet. Then he glanced at Holzer. The damned German was grinning. Malone managed to grin back, then he crawled behind a dead horse and popped away at the Cheyenne rear guard. He saw a cavalry assault repulsed at the edge of the sand dunes, ten men going down before a single barrage from the entrenched Cheyenne.

Kincaid saw the charge, saw the answering fusillade, saw the cavalry charge blunted. He raised an arm and swept it overhead in a commanding motion, and McBride, Holzer, and Chambers formed up on him as he led a sally against the entrenched Cheyennes' flank to cover the cavalry retreat.

They drew a flurry of shots, but as Kincaid reached the dunes and the horses floundered about in the deep sand, the firing halted and the Cheyenne were suddenly gone.

All around them the gunfire ceased, except for an occasional isolated shot. The Cheyenne were gone, vanished into the dunes, which were head-high and better, an impossible badland.

Kincaid sat there, sweat streaming from his face and

153

chest. Then he slowly lowered his pistol, looking for Ketchum. The captain might want pursuit, although it seemed that even Ketchum must see it was impossible. All they would accomplish was to allow themselves to be sniped at for mile upon mile by the Cheyenne rear guard, which would never stay in one position long enough to be attacked themselves. Tactically, Little Wolf had won.

But his men lay scattered across the ground. And to Kincaid's disgust, so did many women and children. "Damn them," he muttered loud enough to be heard by anyone nearby. "Can't they tell the difference?"

He knew it was inevitable. It wasn't Easy Company's doing; he knew his men that well. But Ketchum's force was made up for the most part of men as green as new peas. Frightened, they had fired on everyone not wearing blue.

He found Ketchum, his face blackened by powder smoke, looking dazed. He still held his pistol in his hand, and almost in confusion he stared across the field littered with broken bodies. Nearly at his feet, a sergeant with a badly shot-up leg was being tended to. It didn't look like he was going to make it.

"Pursuit, sir?" Kincaid asked.

"No." Ketchum shook his head. "We can't dig them out of there. Let's take what we have." He nodded toward Dull Knife's band, which stood impassively watching.

"Into Robinson?" Kincaid asked. To begin the whole futile cycle over again. To Robinson and then to the Nation, where another breakout would be planned.

"Robinson," Ketchum substantiated with a nod. He had noticed the look on Kincaid's face, and he suddenly shouted, "Damn it, Kincaid, I'm only a soldier too!"

"I know it, sir," Kincaid said, at that moment feeling deep sympathy for the captain. He was in over his depth, and as he said, he was only a man trying to do his duty. In the face of Little Wolf's warmaking, what else was there to do? He rested a hand briefly on Ketchum's shoulder. "That's the whole trouble, isn't it? We're only soldiers."

The march to Robinson was a tragedy. Wounded men fell by the wayside, dying in agony. Women and children, some carrying bullets, were left at the side of the road. Ketchum looked like living hell. Perhaps he felt responsible for all of it. His cheeks were hollow, his hands trembling, his eyes sunken and lost.

Robinson looked like a death camp by the time they reached it, hungry, wounded, and battered. Kincaid had to make most of the report to Colonel Danner, who took it all in with equanimity.

"Looks like we'll have to pen them up here for the winter. I can't see anyone marching south, in the condition they're in. I'll get my Sioux trackers out after Little Wolf. Don't worry, the Sioux could find a dune rat by full darkness."

Kincaid only nodded. Right then he didn't give a damn whether they got Little Wolf or not, although his logical mind told him that the man was rabid now, striking out at anything white that lay in his path. His concern lay more with the peacemaker, Dull Knife.

"Is there no way they can stay in the north, sir? To send them back to Reno . . . they'll die there, sir, of broken hearts. Dull Knife's a man of peace, or he tried to be. How much more can he take?"

"That's not my decision, Kincaid," Danner said abruptly. "Nor yours," he reminded him unnecessarily. Then Danner looked at Frank Ketchum, looked at him long and hard. His voice softened. "Better sack out somewhere, Frank. I'll take care of the details for you."

"You'll wire Reno?" he asked without lifting his head.

"Yes, of course."

"Then I think I will sack out." He rose, bone weary. Without saluting, he turned and shuffled out of the office.

Danner looked at Kincaid, finding his eyes hard, his face immobile.

"Same goes for you, Kincaid."

"What will you do with Dull Knife?"

"We've got a row of condemned barracks. They'll be housed there. Can't leave them outside now, can I?"

"No, sir." Kincaid had seen those barracks. They had been designed for fifty troopers. Dull Knife's band numbered a hundred and eleven people. But there was nothing to be done, nothing to be gained by speaking up. "Will you wire Number Nine as well, sir?"

"Already have. Unfortunately your captain's in the field."

"I see." Kincaid nodded slowly, feeling weariness pummeling him. His eyelids weighed a ton, his muscles were drawn thin, stiff and knotted. His head was filled with a dry gray haze.

"Get some sleep, Kincaid. You've done all you can."

"And it wasn't a hell of a lot, was it, sir?" Kincaid demanded.

He saluted then and walked from the room, Danner's burning eyes on his back. He found the BOQ and flopped onto the nearest bunk without determining whether it belonged to someone. He didn't bother to remove his boots or unstrap his gunbelt.

He closed his eyes, expecting sleep, but his mind stayed on the ragged edge of consciousness, and through the haze of his weary thoughts he was aware of sounds. Commands, shouts, a high wailing, a baby's cry, someone chanting the Cheyenne death song.

Was it morning or night? Kincaid was awake, but his eyes were closed. It was a long minute before he could recall who he was, what reality was, where he now lay. He clawed at his eyes and sat up, his blood forcing its way through his blood vessels. He was heavy with sleep, like a man who has been on a drinking binge.

He forced an eye open, saw that the room was darker

than it should be during daylight, and looked around. The BOQ was empty, which told him it was still early. He sat there, head hanging, hands on the edge of the bunk, for a long minute. Suddenly he remembered, and he made an effort to rise.

Stretch Dobbs had been carried in on a travois. That motivated Kincaid to struggle to his feet and find a water basin with water left in it, shave by the dim light of a lantern and, straightening his wrinkled tunic as well as possible, go out into the night.

It was still early. In the sutler's store, men were drinking beer. Some of them had spilled out onto the plankwalk. They spoke in loud voices, moving their arms animatedly.

There was a light in the day room, another in the orderly room. Kincaid stood for a minute, breathing in the fresh cold air, then started toward the infirmary.

"Yes?" A man with a dark goatee looked up from a ledger.

"You have one of my men. Private Dobbs?"

The surgeon's expression darkened and Kincaid felt his heart skip, but the doctor said, "He's improving."

"May I see him?"

"You may, but he won't see you. I gave him morphine for the pain, he'll be out for twenty-four hours."

Kincaid was shown into the hospital, and he smiled as he identified Stretch instantly by the bare feet protruding from under the sheets.

The doctor spoke in a low voice. He had been busy that evening, and the strain showed. His hospital was filled, every bed, much of the floor space.

"He took the bullet high, and it passed under the collar bone." The doctor tapped his own chest, indicating the spot. "The exit took a portion of the scapula, the wing bone, with it, but he's in no danger, at least I hope not. Probably a month's rest will take care of everything. He's a young, vigorous man."

Then he studied Kincaid thoughtfully. "You know,

Lieutenant, I could give you a sleeping powder. Frankly, you look unwell. You were with Captain Ketchum?" Kincaid nodded and the doctor motioned him aside. Ketchum lay in a bunk, his pale face strained even in drugged sleep.

"Fatigue, tension. It can do terrible things to a soldier," the doctor said.

"Yes. I'll be all right. Thank you, sir." Kincaid stuck out his hand and the doctor took it.

Outside, the night was turning cold. It was late in the year, and soon those Nebraska plains would be raked by cold winds; the snow would be deep along the Niobrara, and all war would cease.

He thought briefly of Little Wolf, wondered about Danner's plan, and then mentally smashed the thoughts. He refused to think about battle, refused to let his eyes drift toward the low line of decrepit barracks outside the walls of Fort Robinson.

Instead, straightening his shoulders, he walked toward the sutler's store, passing some of Easy Company without really noticing them.

Norm Braun looked up with surprise and shock. "Kincaid! You look like hell, man. Sit down. I've got a ham and a cheese cut in the back. Let me give you something."

"Do you have whiskey?" Matt asked, sagging into a chair.

"You know I'm not allowed to sell whiskey."

"Ham and cheese, then, Mr. Braun. Thanks."

The sutler was gone for a few minutes. After looking around the room for a while, watching the talking soldiers, he rested his head on his forearms, closing his eyes.

"Is the kitchen closed?" asked a harsh, familiar voice, and Kincaid's head came up. Katie was there, and despite the tone of voice, she was smiling. The smile faded as she got a good look at Kincaid. "Good Lord!" she breathed.

"That for me?" he asked, and she nodded, placing the platter covered with thick slabs of ham and generous slices of Cheddar before him. From her apron she produced a bottle of labeled whiskey.

"Someone left this here," she said.

"Tell your uncle thanks," Kincaid said with a weak smile. He pulled the cork and filled a tumbler full of whiskey. He drank it down, feeling the flood of warmth through his stomach and lungs, feeling his skin flush.

He drained the glass and then began to eat, the whiskey having roused his appetite. A chair scraped against the floor, and with surprise, Matt saw that Katie Braun had seated herself opposite him.

He continued to eat, aware of her eyes on him, aware of her soft fragrance. He tried to pay it no attention, knowing she wanted none.

When he was through, he poured another glass of whiskey and drank it slowly. "Do you feel like talking?" Katie asked. "I mean . . . God, Matt, you look terrible."

"War is terrible," he reminded her. He said nothing else, rebuffing her attempts to draw him out of himself. When his stomach was full, when the whiskey had unknotted his muscles, he felt himself begin to sag. He wanted nothing so much as to sleep. To sleep deeply, dreamlessly. He glanced at Katie, whose eyes sparkled in the lantern light, and smiled weakly.

"I'll be all right. No need for you to stay."

"You look all right," she replied ironically. "You belong in bed, if not in the hospital."

"In bed," Matt replied. He smiled sleepily. "I don't know if I can get up."

It was true. His legs had gone leaden, his mind was back in that gray haze. Too much whiskey, too many miles.

"I don't want to find out," he went on. "I don't want to lurch around, fall on my face. The men will think I'm drunk," he said with a nod toward the group of enlisted men. "What else could they think?"

"You'd rather sit there all night?"

"If I can. Until they're gone. Maybe you could ask your uncle..." His mouth broke open in a tremendous yawn, which filled his eyes with tears. He hid the yawn behind a fist and smiled an apology.

"This is ridiculous, Lieutenant Kincaid," Katie said sharply. "There's a room in the back. Go into the storeroom and turn right. You'll see a small alcove and a door."

"I couldn't bother you."

"I won't have soldiers dying in here," she said, "and that's what you're setting yourself up for. To die of exhaustion."

"It's just that the whiskey hit me a little hard. I'll be on my way..." His chin dropped to his chest, and his eyes closed.

"Come on." She put her hand under his arm, and Kincaid blinked his eyes open. "I'll walk you to the back."

"What'll people think?" Matt asked with a sly smile.

"As if I cared!" she snapped, not knowing that he was joking.

He went along with her, she carrying a good deal of his weight. "This is good of you. Just an hour and I'll be fine."

"I'll bet." They passed through the darkened storeroom, and Katie fished for a key over the sill of the small room beyond. Opening the door, she led him in.

"In a hour or so—"

"Oh, shut up, Kincaid!" she said, though there was no trace of anger in the exclamation. Matt felt himself lowered onto a bed, and he heard her rustling around in the darkness for a while. Then she was gone, the door closing gently behind her, and he smiled.

The bed was soft, the room dark and completely silent, separated as it was from the store. He could see nothing of the room in the darkness, but there was a faint telltale something that identified it as a woman's room. The vague scent of perfume, perhaps, so slight as to be just beneath the level of conscious registration. The softness of the bedspread, the warm aura of the place. There was no doubt whose room it was, and he smiled again before breaking into a prodigious yawn. This was quite a remarkable step for Katie Braun—allowing a man to sleep in her bed.

Kincaid did sleep, this time deeply and soundly. Yet sometime before dawn, something triggered his soldier's instinct, that instinct which keeps a man alive in the field.

Something. A sound...? He opened his eye only a hair, noticing the room was still utterly dark. Then he heard a sound, silky, soft sound like wind in the trees, and he saw the dark silhouette draw nearer.

Katie. Her hands went to his waist and she unbuttoned his pants. Going to the end of the bed, she grabbed his cuffs and pulled, tugging his pants off.

He thought, *She's trying to make me more comfortable,* and was careful not to stir to show her he was awake. Poor thing would probably go through the ceiling.

That was what he thought until she returned to stand over him, and he could hear her breathing, deep and quick. *My God,* he thought, *this is a vivid dream.*

Vivid it was. The dream hovered over him a while longer, and then stretched out gentle hands, hands that found his penis and lifted it gently, measuring it, handling it with awe. That sound—Kincaid realized what it was as dawn light filtered in from some chink high on the wall. Katie Braun, her dark hair loose about her shoulders, had slipped out of her clothes, and now stood there naked, her beautiful figure silhouetted against the dark wall, only a shade lighter.

Her breasts were full—he had never noticed how full before, bound up as they were, and her hair was a silky, waving veil. And her hands! She still held him, and Kincaid was aware of the growing erection, the hot flow of blood as she thoughtfully turned it over, gripping it lightly as if to measure its girth.

161

What do I do? Kincaid wondered. *Stay asleep. There's nothing else to do.* He didn't want to risk chasing her away. Her critical examination, the soft probing and measuring, were excruciatingly pleasant.

What now? Her hand ran up across his hard abdomen to his shirt and she slowly unbottoned it, her lips following along until she had bared his chest.

Then, unexpectedly, she straddled him. He felt the silky brush of her thigh against his, felt a momentary soft dampness, and then she leaned far forward, her breasts grazing his chest, and kissed his lips.

"Are you asleep?" she asked, and her voice was different—softer, deeper, huskier.

"How could I be?" Matt replied. He didn't want to say anything else, didn't want to break the spell.

Her lips touched his, delicately, deliberately, parting just enough to surround his lower lip. Her breath was warm against his cheek. She moved from side to side slightly, her nipples grazing his chest.

Nobody but a corpse could have pretended to be unmoved, and Kincaid gave up on lying still, letting her have her way, satisfying her curiosity as if he were an anatomical model.

He reached up and pulled her mouth to his, kissing her hard. His other hand roamed down across the swale of her back and up along the rise of her magnificent hips.

She responded eagerly now. She kissed his throat, his ears, his eyelids, and her body began a rhythmic, unaccustomed thrusting.

"Oh, Matt. My goodness. Goodness," she murmured, and he kissed her again, finding her mouth open to meet his, her lips soft and busy.

He let his fingers slip between her thighs, and she gasped, reflexively closing her legs, but as his probing fingers continued their work, as the heat from his kisses increased the hot trickle inside of her, she spread them again, allowing his fingers to dip inside, exploring the tantalizing contours of her body.

"Matt!" She lifted her head and her eyes were dazed,

almost as if he had stunned her with some shocking blow. She buried her head against his chest, her hair spilling across him, and she lifted herself up onto her knees, letting him probe her more easily, more deeply.

Her mouth was against his chest, and she murmured a series of instructions, instructions impossible to ignore. "I'd like it a little deeper, feel that ridge. Yes. My goodness, my goodness!" She lifted herself slightly and cupped her breasts in her hands. "Will you kiss my breasts? Hold them! Kiss the nipples, Matt. My, they feel electric. When you do that, I can feel it clear through my head!"

She talked more than any woman Matt had been in bed with, but far from being distracting, he found it exciting.

"It's so big, hot, and heavy, and I can feel it throbbing. You can tell there's something inside that has to be let go. Smoldering and . . . does that feel good? Do you like me to run my fingers over the tip . . . oh, that's awfully sensitive, isn't it? What if I just rub it against me there, where your finger is. Oh, Matt . . . !"

She had begun to move her hips, to sway from side to side, and Matt knew there was something inside of her that had to be released as well.

Reaching down, she grabbed his erection, and spreading herself, she lifted her hips and settled onto him with a gratified shudder.

Sitting up, she placed her hands on his abdomen and began to sway dreamily, lifting herself no more than an inch before grinding herself against him. Her hands kneaded his stomach like a cat's paws. Her head lolled on her neck as if it were too heavy to support, and her eyes, half closed, were distant and glassy as she began to work more emphatically against him, to accentuate her thrusting, to lengthen and intensify her strokes.

She talked constantly, triggering Matt's responses. "That's good. Yes. Now a little more . . . yes, and higher and harder, and harder!"

Her voice fell away into a stream of meaningless syllables as her hips worked with an untrained virtuosity, swinging in wide, soft arcs, drawing him into her, driving with a demanding motion for which there were no more words, but only the savage rhythm, the moist coupling, the soft sounds, the hot points of intensity where nerve rubbed against nerve until all reserve buckled and all restraint was washed away in the white-hot, onrushing flood.

She shrieked and sat bolt upright, flinging her head back, biting at her lower lip, gripping her own breasts tightly at Matt arched his back and thrust deeply into her, dividing her, battering her, threatening to split her open until he reached his own climax with a final shuddering motion and she collapsed against him, clawing at him, kissing his shoulders, chest, face, and neck as her hands roamed his body, as her moist breath fanned out across his exhausted body.

And then she was still and he held her, feeling the soft, unconscious draining of their bodies, the tiny spasms. He held her and stroked that fine dark hair and kissed her cheek, bringing a smile to her lips, a deeply satisfied, proud smile. He hugged her tightly and they slept for a time, content and weary.

The footsteps outside the door brought them alert with a start.

"Is the door locked?" Matt asked.

"Nobody can get in. God, what time is it?"

It was no longer dark out; Matt could see a narrow ribbon of light against the rough plank wall of the tiny room, and he sat up as Katie slipped from the bed and crept to the door, listening.

"It's just a load of corn being delivered," she said, nervously arranging her undone hair. Her eyes gave him his cue. Eyes that looked startled, amazed, shying away from his naked body.

"I guess I'd better slip out anyway, hadn't I?"

"Yes." She nodded gratefully and then, realizing she too was naked, searched for and found a pale blue wrapper, which she wound herself in.

164

Matt got into his clothes and returned to the door. Katie had opened it an inch and was peering out. Matt slipped his arms around her and kissed the nape of her neck. "Maybe I'd better wait until it's dark," he whispered.

"No," she laughed, then added seriously, "but maybe you'd better come back after dark. You know where the key is now."

He nodded and hugged her again, but she pulled away. "Now. They've closed the back door again. You can slip out."

"But I don't want to go."

"I know, darling, but you must. That's got to be an order."

"Every way I turn, orders!"

He kissed her again, briefly, and then slipped out of her door and into the storeroom, finding it temporarily empty. He moved to the back door, slipped the latch, and was out. He walked slowly toward the gate, liking the chill air, the fresh light of morning, the scent of dew on the grass. By God, the world could be good, every sight and scent of it, all the small things—trees in the wind, the slant of sunlight through the clouds. And then he saw the old barracks, guarded heavily by cavalry, and his high spirits flattened and curled in upon themselves.

Was Dull Knife peering out of one of those greasy, boarded windows, praying for help, wondering what sins he had committed?

It was possible, and Kincaid said silently, "Sorry, old boy. There's not a damned thing I can do to help you. Not a goddamned thing."

twelve _____

The weather turned bitterly cold. The winds from out of the northwest howled across the plains, and the snows fell. The Easy Company detachment at Fort Robinson was restless. They still had not been released by Danner, who claimed he needed them to help guard the Cheyenne prisoners, which they did, usually drawing the graveyard shift, when the thermometer had plunged below the zero mark, when the raking winds were at their peak.

Matt Kincaid was in high spirits, and that puzzled everyone but Malone, who had theorized correctly. "He's got a woman, boys."

"Not likely," Wojensky said.

"Oh, but it is." Malone was propped up on his bunk, hands behind his head, still wearing his coat—it was that cold in the barracks, even with the fire going full blast. "Tell me what else could keep a man smiling and whistling in this weather, stuck here?"

"I don't know," Wojensky said doubtfully. "Who, then? There's no women around!"

"There's at least one, and a fine-looking woman too."

"Katie Braun! Don't make me laugh, Malone. That shrew can't stand men, hates soldiers. Y'ever see her smile?"

Malone winked. "No, but I'll bet Kincaid has."

"Wind's stopped," Stretch said. He was standing, peering out the fogged window. "Sky's clearing, but

167

goddamn, it's going to be a cold shift. Anybody seen the thermometer?"

"Why look?" Reb replied. "It only discourages a man."

"Tell you what discourages *me,*" Dubois said from his corner bunk, "being here at Robinson. By God, we're just as much prisoners as the Cheyenne. Penned up with cavalry!" he said with disgust, as if there could be no more vile torture.

"Well, it beats hell out of the way they're treating the Cheyenne," McBride replied.

"How so?"

"I'm telling you, those people are starving."

"Bullshit!" Dubois scoffed. "Army wouldn't let 'em starve."

"What you mean," McBride corrected, "is that *you* wouldn't let 'em, *I* wouldn't let 'em. Kincaid or Conway, *they* wouldn't. What *I'm* sayin' is that they *are* starving. You ever see food go in those barracks? Or water?"

"Not on the graveyard shift," Dubois said logically.

"No, then how about heat? You ever see smoke coming out of those stovepipes? There ain't any, because Landers is afraid they'll burn the place down."

Dubois thought about that for a while, then he looked toward the frozen window in their own barracks and was silent. McBride met Malone's eyes, then shifted away.

The son of a bitch is right, Malone thought. *Damned if he ain't.* Malone decided that he was blind himself not to have noticed, but when he was walking night guard, his only thought had been for his own warmth, as he stamped his feet and slapped his arms, fighting off the numbing cold of Nebraska winter. He just hadn't thought about it, but he was thinking now, thinking about Dawn Cloud and old Dull Knife, and that kid Holzer had befriended. Slowly starving, slowly freezing . . . he turned over suddenly on his bunk, trying to sleep, but the images would not go away.

"I'll see about that," he muttered, and no one answered. Just what in hell was Private Malone going to do? Feed them with his own table scraps, demand food from the CO? He wasn't going to do anything, and they all knew it. There was nothing to be done.

It was cold beyond endurance. Wheeler had stuffed his clothes with straw from the homesteader's barn. He sat hunched over his flickering fire as the cold winds blew.

"What am I doing here? Alone on the Wyoming plains, with winter settling? Crazy, am I? Have I driven myself crazy? I can go in and get stood up before the wall, or stay here and freeze. Deserter. Private Wheeler, deserter." He repeated that several times, liking the sound of it. Then he laughed, a strangled, squeaking laugh. His laughter was cut short by a knife-edge of agony in his guts, churning, burning, doubling him up with pain. He coughed dryly, his shoulders shaking. "Now I'm gonna get pneumonia," he thought.

Maybe if he told them it was self-defense when he killed Mountain Star . . . maybe Conway would have pity on him. If he could only talk to the old man and be sure.

"No, they'd give me hard labor, if they didn't shoot me. Ten years' hard labor . . . but they'd feed me. Maybe a doctor . . ." His guts were on fire, and he closed his eyes with pain. Tears rolled from his eyes, it hurt so badly and the tears froze against his cheeks as the cold wind blasted him.

"Jesus!" he screamed. It was a long, shrill cry to the darkness, the cold and empty night, which broke off into tears. Wheeler stopped abruptly, staring at the fire. There was nothing worse than this. Nothing. Death was better, infinitely better.

He rose stiffly, bent nearly double with the pain in his ravaged stomach. He turned away from the fire, leaving his gun—he would need it no more—and tramped northward, knowing exactly where he was going, exactly what he would do.

Toward midnight the weather cleared, and he saw it

plainly: Outpost Number Nine, sitting dark and isolated against the plains, the scattering of Indian tipis out beyond the deadline. Something burst inside of Wheeler, and with dismay he found himself sobbing. Tears of joy flooded his face.

Tonight there would be a bed, a fire, food. Rest.

He staggered on, leaking straw like a punctured scarecrow, plodding through the blue snow beneath the clear light of a full silver moon.

The guard on the gate was Cantrell. He had been tramping back and forth, chewing on the tail end of a cigar, trying to keep his thoughts anywhere but on his situation here. It was cold, cold enough to freeze a man's bones. He hunched his shoulders, buried his hands in his coat, and turned again. And then he saw it and he blinked, shaking his head. He had to be imagining it, but he wasn't.

A man afoot, walking through that knee-deep snow toward Number Nine. Who? Cantrell unslung his rifle and watched for a minute, looking behind him toward the sleeping post.

The first thought to present itself was that this was some sort of a trick; the Blodgett episode remained a vivid memory.

Play it cautious, old son, he warned himself. He stood warily watching the man, undecided as to whether or not he should summon help, just in case. But this man, if he was acting, was a hell of an actor.

As he drew nearer, Cantrell could see that he was emaciated, moving with an unsteady, jerky motion, his head hanging. And then, by the moonlight, he could identify the uniform. God, a soldier! Had Conway been hit?

"Who goes there? Who is it!" he called out suddenly, and the head came up and Cantrell nearly dropped his rifle. He had a long beard, hollow eyes, but there was no mistaking the man. He had bunked next to him for ten months.

"Wheeler!"

"Let me in. Please! Let me in, I can't take any more. Let me in!" His voice was broken by sobs, and Cantrell raced for the pole ladder.

The barracks door opened, and Cantrell saw someone rushing toward him: Javitts, in his pants and undershirt, waving a gun.

"What is it? What's the shouting?"

His eyes were wild, and Cantrell knew he had been having those nightmares again. "It's Wheeler," Cantrell told him. "By God and be damned, it's Wheeler. Give me a hand with the gate. Snow's got it blocked."

Frantically they worked, digging the snow away with boots and hands. Together they yanked the gate open, and Cantrell saw Wheeler standing there, hands upraised in salute or surrender or supplication.

"Lord God be praised!" Wheeler shouted. He staggered toward Cantrell, and Javitts shot him three times.

The shots roared in Cantrell's ears. He saw Wheeler slammed back against the snow, blood flowing from his neck, chest, and arm.

Cantrell spun back, looked at Javitts in utter disbelief, and screamed: "What in hell did you do that for? Why? *Why!*"

Men were pouring out of the barracks now. Mr. Taylor, pistol in hand, had burst from the BOQ. Cantrell was leaning over Wheeler, but it was useless. Shot to dog meat. Blood spattered his face and hands. He managed to speak, his voice a ragged whisper.

"I made it back. Guess I don't have to worry about them damned gut aches any longer." Then he attempted a smile, a smile broken off by intense agony. Wheeler was looking at Cantrell, and then he was looking at nothing. His eyes had gone cold. The moonlight glittered in them, and Cantrell turned away angrily.

"You bastard!" He approached Javitts, who was backing up, pistol at his side. "You murdering bastard!"

"I had to do it!" Javitts looked at Cantrell, at Wheeler

171

lying broken on the snow. "I had to do it, you know. He was a deserter! A cowardly deserter. A murderer. Can't take a chance with that kind of man. They'll get you if you don't get them first. It was a trick—all a trick!"

Taylor was there, his hair in his eyes. Surrounding him a half circle, the enlisted men watched with horror as Javitts turned around slowly, his eyes sparkling.

"You've got to do it to them first, Mr. Taylor. They'll kill you. Men like that! A deserter. He was a goddamned deserter! What was I supposed to do? Wait until he raped the captain's wife, until he shot me in the face again? What was I supposed to do!" he screamed, his head thrown back.

He didn't fight as Taylor lifted his gun from his hand. He just stood there, looking at no one, at nothing, until he sank to his knees in the snow and, burying his face in his hands, began to weep.

The cold was a living, malevolent thing that reached through the cracks in the wall and closed around a man, throttling him. The blood slowed, the hands grew numb, the bones creaked, a man's soul grew desolate.

Dull Knife did not speak, no one whispered or shifted. Only the two braves who worked at loosening the floorboards of the barracks moved. The moon was bright on their grim faces as they placed the sections of board aside and lifted the rifles from beneath the floor.

The moon glinted on the rifle barrels and was a pleasing, warming sight. Dull Knife took the cool, friendly instrument into his hands and smiled faintly.

Death. Again he was leading his people into death. Why had he not listened to Little Wolf? Little Wolf's magic was obviously better.

To sit here slowly freezing, slowly starving, having only snow scraped from the windowsills to drink! Better to die free, better to die like a warrior.

Dull Knife crept closer to the window and watched as the bored, cold cavalrymen made their rounds.

He knew precisely how long it took the men to ride their circuit, exactly when the guard was changed. The Cheyenne were bunched behind Dull Knife—the women, the children, the old men. The cavalrymen passed again, and Dull Knife lifted his rifle butt, smashing the boards from the window.

Malone heard shots and sat up. McBride, already dressed in preparation for the graveyard shift, spun toward the window, and the two men looked at each other. It could only be one thing, and Malone shook his head in agony.

"No! Goddammit, no!"

There were footsteps on the plankwalk, and Kincaid burst in.

"Let's go. Dull Knife's broken out."

They sat there for a minute, unable to move. Would this go on forever, until all the Cheyenne were dead?

"I said move!" Kincaid repeated sharply. Then he added, "I know exactly how you feel, boys. I mean that."

It was fifteen minutes before they reached the parade, mounted and ready. Major Halstead, shivering with the cold, was there waiting. The moon was full, bright on the snow.

"They're making for the sand hills, Kincaid," Halstead said. "They shot two sentries—God knows where they had the weapons hidden. I've told my men to shoot to kill."

The gates had been flung open, and the mounted soldiers poured out onto the moonlit plains. The path cut by the Cheyenne was stark and obvious. The soldiers pursued at a dead run.

Malone was praying silently. *Let 'em make it to the sand hills, let 'em be gone.*

But it wasn't to be. The sand hills were no more than half a mile off when they saw the Cheyenne, outlined brightly by the moon—dark, scurrying figures against the snow—and the cavalry opened fire.

Tiny red lances of flame answered their fire, and a

soldier went down beside Malone. They charged on through the bright winter moonlight, firing as they rode forward in a long picket line, and the Indians went down, dying against the snow. The roar of guns, screams of pain and death, the acrid scent of black-powder smoke, the whinnying of horses, and then it was all silence.

The moon continued in its placid course. The snow, clean and fresh, was littered with dark, motionless figures.

Major Halstead's force had continued on. Some of the Cheyenne, Dull Knife included, had made the sand hills. The distant guns popped intermittently. Easy Company remained with the dead and dying.

Kincaid sat his horse, his stomach filled with rising bile. Well, they had done it, finally done it—massacred a people.

Malone staggered among the corpses, and to Kincaid's sickened astonishment, the man fell to his knees beside one of the dead Cheyenne, lifted the head of the corpse to his knee, and screamed, throwing out a stream of violent curses.

"I'm sorry," Kincaid heard him say. He stroked the dead woman's hair, heedless of the eyes upon him. Malone's mouth was drawn down tragically. He looked at McBride and said, "She didn't want me to get hurt, Reb—" A sob broke off his words. McBride could only gawk. That was Malone! Leathery, horn-and-hide Malone, and there were tears flooding his face.

"She didn't want me to get hurt, and so we killed her. I'm sorry, Dawn Cloud. Sorry as hell."

McBride turned away, sick. Holzer was walking numbly across the snowfield, a dead dog in his arms, blood leaking onto the snow.

"Dead dog," Holzer said, presenting it to McBride, and Reb knew there was much bottled up inside of Holzer, but he didn't have the words to say what he felt in English. He simply repeated, "Dead dog," and then turned away, walking from the battle site, and no one tried to stop him.

There were sixty-four corpses on the field; it was Kincaid's job to count them, and so he knew. Sixty-four dead Cheyenne, most of them unarmed. Seventy-eight were recaptured after reaching the dunes, but Dull Knife, his wife, and five members of his family had vanished into the snow-washed sand hills, and Kincaid hoped they were gone for good, that they could return home and never be bound by the white man again.

It was a vain hope. Two weeks later, half frozen, starving, Dull Knife and his family appeared at Robinson and surrendered. The old man was only a sheath of skin over a shattered soul. There was no life in his eyes. His big hands gestured clumsily, helplessly. He didn't even recognize Kincaid the last time he saw him, the day before Easy Company finally rode out of Fort Robinson and rode homeward, returning to Outpost Number Nine.

The day was clear and cold, cleansing—or it should have been, but there were stains that clung. Nothing could wash away the memory of Dull Knife's eyes, nor could riding away from it cause it to fade. Kincaid had never seen his men so silent and withdrawn. Malone spoke to no one, Holzer was disconsolate. There was no laughter, no clowning; he remembered the many times he and Wojensky had disciplined this unruly bunch for their wild behavior. Now he wished they would cut up, turn their hats backward, curse and shout, brawl, get drunk, anything. But they didn't. They couldn't. Not now.

"Maybe in time," Wojensky said, as if reading his lieutenant's thoughts. "Maybe it will just take a little time."

"Maybe." Wojensky was right, of course. Time cures all, Kincaid supposed, but just then, watching his weary, grim men, he wondered just how much time it would take before they could all erase this from their memories.

It was blowing snow, the wind a slicing sword out of the northwest, when Captain Conway pulled his contingent up to await the cavalry troops who were splashing across the icy Little Missouri. Conway had the collar of his greatcoat up, his hat pulled low.

He recognized Captain Wallis, out of Robinson, at the head of the patrol, and also Hudson, out of Laramie. They had three hundred men with them, sixteen Indian scouts, and two Sioux chiefs from the Oglala agency, Hump and Wolf.

"You sure it's them?" Wallis asked without even a greeting or a salute. The man was exhausted, obviously. Hudson looked a trifle better.

"How are you, Warner?"

"William." Conway shook Hudson's hand. Then, to Wallis he said, "It's them. Mandalian, my scout, has spoken to one of them, a cousin of his named Eagle Tree."

"How's it look for them?" Hudson wanted to know, directing his question to Windy, who wore a buffalo coat over his buckskins.

"It's mighty desperate, sir. Eagle Tree says they're starving. He thinks Little Wolf might be ready to throw down the lance. But he'll only do so if the army promises they won't be sent south."

"I am authorized to promise that," Wallis said, his teeth chattering.

His eyes shifted toward the timbered valley below where Little Wolf had his camp. "But will he believe me?" Wallis asked of no one.

"Couldn't blame him if he doesn't," Hudson put in.

"What are we offering?" Conway wanted to know.

"The army will hire them—every mother's son of them—to act as scouts. They can live on the Oglala agency. No tricks, no change in tactics. This is from War." Wallis nodded toward the two Sioux beside him. "We're counting on Hump and Wolf to convince them."

Conway looked at the old Sioux chiefs. He asked Hump, "What will you do?"

The old man's weather-seamed face was expressionless. "We will talk. I am Little Wolf's uncle. I will tell him what the white man offers. Tell him that I believe it is true. Tell him that he must surrender or die. What he will choose, I do not know."

"Let's position our people, then," Hudson said. "Just in case he'd rather die. Though Lord knows I hope he doesn't choose that path."

The troops were positioned by the NCOs. Hudson, Conway, and Wallis sat together on their horses, watching as the old Sioux chiefs disappeared into the valley. The wind was still hard out of the north, and increasing. It was a bad day for fighting, a bad day for dying.

Hours passed, and Conway grew stiff and cold. Then finally they saw something—a patch of color behind the screen of timber—and Conway heard a rifle being cocked. "Hold that," he ordered.

The Sioux reappeared, winding their way up the wooded slope. And they were alone. Conway muttered a slow curse. And then there was someone else, slowly emerging from the timber. A man, and another. A woman carrying a baby. Slowly they came forward, and when they were in clear view of the soldiers, they threw down their weapons.

Little Wolf was at their head, but he had changed. There was no surly anger in his eyes. His face was sunken, and his lips moved spasmodically, soundlessly. He saw Conway, recognized him, and turned his head away in a deliberate gesture.

Conway understood. The man had a right to be bitter, to mistrust all of them. He only hoped that this was the end of the long trail for Little Wolf, that finally the long march was ended and the sadness and dying were finished.

The snow draped the world in white, shifting curtains, the wild winds blew, and the Cheyenne, beaten yet somehow victorious, still proud and strong, were led away between the ranks of blue soldiers.

Conway watched them until they were only vague, colorless blurs against the backdrop of snow, then he

177

turned to Gus Olsen and said, "Let's turn them for home, Gus."

Kincaid had arrived two days earlier, just before the big blizzard set in, and Conway greeted him warmly in his office, surprised at the loss of weight Matt had suffered, the nearly grateful smile that spread over his face as he greeted his commanding officer.

"God, it's good to see you, sir," Kincaid said, sagging into a chair, accepting a glass of bourbon. "It seemed as if we would never get home."

"The whole episode was one I'd like to forget, Matt. Frankly, it gave me cause to wonder. I'm a soldier first and always, but it made me consider my role. It was nasty, couldn't have been much nastier."

"But for Little Wolf it worked out. For him, for seventy-five of his people. They're army scouts, well paid, well housed, free."

"For Little Wolf, yes. But for Dull Knife . . . well, his people were sent back to the Pine Ridge agency, except for the handful who agreed to go back to Reno. And what a homecoming that must have been, what humiliation, to be returned to the Nation."

"Thank God I wasn't there to see it, or to see Dull Knife being taken to Pine Ridge. Closely guarded, a dangerous man." Kincaid smiled thinly and drained his whiskey glass.

"Well," Conway offered, "at least he didn't have to go back to the Nation."

"No." Matt was thoughtful. "But the cost, sir. The cost of it all!"

"I know. And what did we teach them?" Conway refilled their glasses. "Little Wolf, who fought, who killed whites, who forced them to offer peace terms, was granted a pardon and given a job as scout for the army."

Conway sighed, turning to look out the window at the snowy plains. "And Dull Knife, who wanted peace, who gave in at every crucial point, was locked up and forced

178

to kill finally, and is now fenced in at the agency. So what indeed did we teach them, Matt? That making war, dealing from strength, is the better option? You tell me."

"I can't, sir," Matt replied. "I think now there's nothing to be said about it, nothing to be done. We only have to forget," he said, as if any of them ever could.

"Did you hear about Wheeler?" Conway asked.

"It's the talk of the post. Will be all winter, I suppose."

"I wonder what we did to Javitts, what we taught him. That he had to kill to survive, that he would be rewarded for killing. We made a killer out of him."

Conway turned back from the window. He placed his glass on his desk and shook his head. "There's not much going on, with the weather like it is. I do need someone to ride through to Fort Robinson and bring back that horse herd. Dirty job in this cold. Mr. Taylor is elected, I guess; he's been cooling his heels for some time."

"I wouldn't mind doing it, sir," Kincaid said, and Conway frowned.

"I wouldn't think of it, Matt. I know how much you hate Fort Robinson, and you haven't slept in a bunk much lately. Weather's nasty. I'll send Taylor."

"Really, sir," Matt said, rising. "I would like the job. I'd like to volunteer."

"For Fort Robinson?" Conway studied his lieutenant. What in the world could compel Kincaid to go back there, ever?

"Yes, sir. The weather doesn't bother me, and if it gets bad enough . . . well, we could hole up there for a month or so."

"Whatever you say, Matt," Conway answered hesitantly. "If you want the job, you're welcome to it. I'm sure Mr. Taylor won't complain."

"Good." Kincaid nodded. "I'll round up some volunteers and be on my way."

"Today?" Conway asked, lifting an eyebrow. Matt was nearly to the door already, and he nodded.

"As good a time as any."

179

He had that strange, distant look in his eyes again, that wistful smile, which Fitzgerald had been inclined to blame on a woman. Conway shook his head, wondering about Matt. Maybe he had been on the plains too long, but what an officer, accepting a job like this one! Noble self-sacrifice. That was Kincaid.

"Sergeant Cohen!" Conway called. "How about a cup of fresh coffee?"

"Yes, sir!" Cohen boomed.

Warner Conway sat wondering about Matt Kincaid a minute longer, then he turned to the piles of reports that had stacked up on his desk, and with a cup of fresh hot coffee at his elbow, he got to work.

Watch for

EASY COMPANY AND THE BOOTLEGGERS

the next novel in Jove's exciting
High Plains adventure series

EASY COMPANY

coming in June!

Ride the High Plains with the rough-and-tumble Infantrymen of Outpost Nine—in John Wesley Howard's EASY COMPANY series!

____05761-4	EASY COMPANY AND THE SUICIDE BOYS #1	$1.95
____05804-1	EASY COMPANY AND THE MEDICINE GUN #2	$1.95
____05887-4	EASY COMPANY AND THE GREEN ARROWS #3	$1.95
____05945-5	EASY COMPANY AND THE WHITE MAN'S PATH #4	$1.95
____05946-3	EASY COMPANY AND THE LONGHORNS #5	$1.95
____05947-1	EASY COMPANY AND THE BIG MEDICINE #6	$1.95
____05948-X	EASY COMPANY IN THE BLACK HILLS #7	$1.95
____05950-1	EASY COMPANY ON THE BITTER TRAIL #8	$1.95
____05951-X	EASY COMPANY IN COLTER'S HELL #9	$1.95
____06030-5	EASY COMPANY AND THE	
	HEADLINE HUNTER #10	$1.95
____05950-1	EASY COMPANY ON THE BITTER TRAIL #11	$1.95
____05953-6	EASY COMPANY AND THE BLOODY FLAG #12	$1.95

Bestselling Books
for Today's Reader —
From Jove!